James and the Giant Peach

PUFFIN BOOKS BY ROALD DAHL

The BFG
Boy: Tales of Childhood
Charlie and the Chocolate Factory
Charlie and the Great Glass Elevator
Danny, the Champion of the World
Dirty Beasts
The Enormous Crocodile
Esio Trot
Fantastic Mr. Fox
George's Marvelous Medicine
The Giraffe and the Pelly and Me
Going Solo
James and the Giant Peach
The Magic Finger
Matilda
The Minpins
Roald Dahl's Revolting Recipes
Roald Dahl's Revolting Rhymes
The Twits
The Vicar of Nibbleswicke
The Witches
The Wonderful Story of Henry Sugar and Six More

JAMES and the GIANT PEACH

A Children's Story

— ※ —

ROALD DAHL

ILLUSTRATED BY LANE SMITH

PUFFIN BOOKS

PUFFIN BOOKS
Published by the Penguin Group
Penguin Books USA Inc., 375 Hudson Street, New York, New York 10014, U.S.A.
Penguin Books Ltd, 27 Wrights Lane, London W8 5TZ, England
Penguin Books Australia Ltd, Ringwood, Victoria, Australia
Penguin Books Canada Ltd, 10 Alcorn Avenue, Toronto, Ontario, Canada M4V 3B2
Penguin Books (N.Z.) Ltd, 182–190 Wairau Road, Auckland 10, New Zealand

Penguin Books Ltd, Registered Offices: Harmondsworth, Middlesex, England

First published in the United States of America by Alfred A. Knopf, Inc., 1961
First published in Puffin Books, 1988
This edition published simultaneously by Alfred A. Knopf, Inc., and
Puffin Books, 1996

The Library of Congress has cataloged the previous Puffin
edition under catalog card number: 88-42879
This edition ISBN 0-14-037424-8

Book designed by Molly Leach

Printed in the United States of America

This book
is for *Olivia* and *Tessa*

James and the Giant Peach

I

HERE is James Henry Trotter when he was about four years old.

Up until this time, he had had a happy life, living peacefully with his mother and father in a beautiful house beside the sea. There were always plenty of other children for him to play with, and there was the sandy beach for him to run about on, and the ocean to paddle in. It was the perfect life for a small boy.

Then, one day, James's mother and father went to London to do some shopping, and there a terrible thing happened. Both of them suddenly got eaten up (in full daylight, mind you, and on a crowded street) by an enormous angry rhinoceros which had escaped from the London Zoo.

Now this, as you can well imagine, was a rather nasty experience for two such gentle parents. But in the long run it was far nastier for James than it was for them. *Their* troubles were all over in a jiffy. They were dead and gone in thirty-five seconds flat. Poor James, on the other hand, was still very much alive, and all at once he found himself alone and frightened in a vast unfriendly world. The lovely house by the seaside had to be sold immediately, and the little boy, carrying nothing but a small suitcase containing a pair of pajamas and a toothbrush, was sent away to live with his two aunts.

Their names were Aunt Sponge and Aunt Spiker, and I am sorry to say that they were both really horrible people. They were selfish and lazy and cruel, and right from the beginning they started beating poor James for almost no reason at all. They never called him by his real name, but always referred to him as "you disgusting little beast" or "you filthy nuisance" or "you miserable creature," and they certainly never gave him any toys to play with or any picture books to look at. His room was as bare as a prison cell.

They lived—Aunt Sponge, Aunt Spiker, and now James as well—in a queer ramshackle house on the top of a high hill in the south of England. The hill was so high that from almost anywhere in the garden James could look down and see for

miles and miles across a marvelous landscape of woods and fields; and on a very clear day, if he looked in the right direction, he could see a tiny gray dot far away on the horizon, which was the house that he used to live in with his beloved mother and father. And just beyond that, he could see the ocean itself—a long thin streak of blackish-blue, like a line of ink, beneath the rim of the sky.

But James was never allowed to go down off the top of that hill. Neither Aunt Sponge nor Aunt Spiker could ever be bothered to take him out herself, not even for a small walk or a picnic, and he certainly wasn't permitted to go alone. "The nasty little beast will only get into mischief if he goes out of the garden," Aunt Spiker had said. And terrible punishments were promised him, such as being locked up in the cellar with the rats for a week, if he even so much as dared to climb over the fence.

The garden, which covered the whole of the top of the hill, was large and desolate, and the only tree in the entire place (apart from a clump of dirty old laurel bushes at the far end) was an ancient peach tree that never gave any peaches. There was no swing, no seesaw, no sand pit, and no other children were ever invited to come up the hill to play with poor James. There wasn't so much as a dog or a cat around to keep him company. And as time went on, he became sadder and sadder, and more and more lonely, and he used to spend hours every day standing at the bottom of the garden, gazing wistfully at the lovely but forbidden world of woods and fields and ocean that was spread out below him like a magic carpet.

2

Here is James Henry Trotter after he had been living with his aunts for three whole years—which is when this story really begins.

For now, there came a morning when something rather peculiar happened to him. And this thing, which as I say was only *rather* peculiar, soon caused a second thing to happen which was *very* peculiar. And then the *very* peculiar thing, in its own turn, caused a really *fantastically* peculiar thing to occur.

It all started on a blazing hot day in the middle of summer. Aunt Sponge, Aunt Spiker, and James were all out in the garden. James had been put to work, as usual. This time he was chopping wood for the kitchen stove. Aunt Sponge and Aunt Spiker were sitting comfortably in deck-chairs nearby, sipping tall glasses of fizzy lemonade and watching him to see that he didn't stop work for one moment.

Aunt Sponge was enormously fat and very short. She had small piggy eyes, a sunken mouth, and one of those white flabby faces that looked exactly as though it had been boiled. She was like a great white soggy overboiled cabbage. Aunt Spiker, on the other hand, was lean and tall and bony, and she wore steel-rimmed spectacles that fixed onto the end of her nose with a clip. She had a screeching voice and long wet narrow lips, and whenever she got angry or excited, little flecks of spit would come shooting out of her mouth as she talked. And there they sat, these two ghastly hags, sipping their drinks, and every now and again screaming at James to chop faster and faster. They also talked about themselves, each one saying how beautiful she thought she was. Aunt Sponge had a long-handled mirror on her lap, and she kept picking it up and gazing at her own hideous face.

> *"I look and smell," Aunt Sponge declared, "as*
> *lovely as a rose!*
> *Just feast your eyes upon my face, observe my*
> *shapely nose!*
> *Behold my heavenly silky locks!*
> *And if I take off both my socks*
> *You'll see my dainty toes."*
> *"But don't forget," Aunt Spiker cried, "how much*
> *your tummy shows!"*

> *Aunt Sponge went red. Aunt Spiker said, "My sweet,*
> *you cannot win,*
> *Behold* MY *gorgeous curvy shape, my teeth, my*
> *charming grin!*

Oh, beauteous me! How I adore
My radiant looks! And please ignore
The pimple on my chin."
"My dear old trout!" Aunt Sponge cried out,
    "You're only bones and skin!"

"Such loveliness as I possess can only truly shine
In Hollywood!" Aunt Sponge declared. "Oh,
    wouldn't that be fine!
I'd capture all the nations' hearts!
They'd give me all the leading parts!
The stars would all resign!"
"I think you'd make," Aunt Spiker said, "a lovely
    Frankenstein."

Poor James was still slaving away at the chopping-block.
The heat was terrible. He was sweating all over. His arm was
aching. The chopper was a large blunt thing far too heavy for a
small boy to use. And as he worked, James began thinking
about all the other children in the world and what they might
be doing at this moment. Some would be riding tricycles in
their gardens. Some would be walking in cool woods and picking bunches of wild flowers. And all the little friends whom he
used to know would be down by the seaside, playing in the wet
sand and splashing around in the water...

Great tears began oozing out of James's eyes and rolling
down his cheeks. He stopped working and leaned against the
chopping-block, overwhelmed by his own unhappiness.

"What's the matter with you?" Aunt Spiker screeched, glaring at him over the top of her steel spectacles.

James began to cry.

"Stop that immediately and get on with your work, you nasty little beast!" Aunt Sponge ordered.

"Oh, Auntie Sponge!" James cried out. "And Auntie Spiker! Couldn't we all—*please*—just for once—go down to the seaside on the bus? It isn't very far—and I feel so hot and awful and lonely…"

"Why, you lazy good-for-nothing brute!" Aunt Spiker shouted.

"Beat him!" cried Aunt Sponge.

"I certainly will!" Aunt Spiker snapped. She glared at James, and James looked back at her with large frightened eyes. "I shall beat you later on in the day when I don't feel so hot," she said. "And now get out of my sight, you disgusting little worm, and give me some peace!"

James turned and ran. He ran off as fast as he could to the far end of the garden and hid himself behind that clump of dirty old laurel bushes that we mentioned earlier on. Then he covered his face with his hands and began to cry and cry.

3

It was at this point that the first thing of all, the *rather* peculiar thing that led to so many other *much* more peculiar things, happened to him.

For suddenly, just behind him, James heard a rustling of leaves, and he turned around and saw an old man in a crazy dark-green suit emerging from the bushes. He was a very small old man, but he had a huge bald head and a face that was cov-

ered all over with bristly black whiskers. He stopped when he was about three yards away, and he stood there leaning on his stick and staring hard at James.

When he spoke, his voice was very slow and creaky. "Come closer to me, little boy," he said, beckoning to James with a finger. "Come right up close to me and I will show you something *wonderful*."

James was too frightened to move.

The old man hobbled a step or two nearer, and then he put a hand into the pocket of his jacket and took out a small white paper bag.

"You see this?" he whispered, waving the bag gently to and

fro in front of James's face. "You know what this is, my dear? You know what's inside this little bag?"

Then he came nearer still, leaning forward and pushing his face so close to James that James could feel breath blowing on his cheeks. The breath smelled musty and stale and slightly mildewed, like air in an old cellar.

"Take a look, my dear," he said, opening the bag and tilting it toward James. Inside it, James could see a mass of tiny green things that looked like little stones or crystals, each one about the size of a grain of rice. They were extraordinarily beautiful, and there was a strange brightness about them, a sort of luminous quality that made them glow and sparkle in the most wonderful way.

"Listen to them!" the old man whispered. "Listen to them move!"

James stared into the bag, and sure enough there was a faint rustling sound coming up from inside it, and then he noticed that all the thousands of little green things were slowly, very very slowly stirring about and moving over each other as though they were alive.

"There's more power and magic in those things in there than in all the rest of the world put together," the old man said softly.

"But—but—what *are* they?" James murmured, finding his voice at last. "Where do they come from?"

"Ah-ha," the old man whispered. "You'd never guess that!" He was crouching a little now and pushing his face still closer and closer to James until the tip of his long nose was actually touching the skin on James's forehead. Then suddenly he jumped back and began waving his stick madly in the air. "Crocodile tongues!" he cried. "One thousand long slimy crocodile tongues boiled up in the skull of a dead witch for twenty days and nights with the eyeballs of a lizard! Add the fingers of a young monkey, the gizzard of a pig, the beak of a green parrot, the juice of a porcupine, and three spoonfuls of sugar. Stew for another week, and then let the moon do the rest!"

All at once, he pushed the white paper bag into James's hands, and said, "Here! You take it! It's yours!"

4

James Henry Trotter stood there clutching the bag and staring at the old man.

"And now," the old man said, "all you've got to do is this. Take a large jug of water, and pour all the little green things into it. Then, very slowly, one by one, add ten hairs from your own head. That sets them off! It gets them going! In a couple of minutes the water will begin to froth and bubble furiously, and as soon as that happens you must quickly drink it all down, the whole jugful, in one gulp. And then, my dear, you will feel it churning and boiling in your stomach, and steam will start coming out of your mouth, and immediately after that, *marvelous* things will start happening to you, *fabulous, unbelievable* things—and you will never be miserable again in your life. Because you *are* miserable, aren't you? You needn't tell me! I know *all* about it! Now, off you go and do exactly as I say. And don't whisper a word of this to those two horrible aunts of yours! Not a word! And don't let those green things in there get away from you either! Because if they do escape, then they will be working their magic upon somebody else instead of upon *you*! And that isn't what you want at all, is it, my dear? *Whoever they meet first, be it bug, insect, animal, or tree, that will be the one who gets the full power of their magic!* So hold the bag tight! Don't tear the paper! Off you go! Hurry up! Don't wait! Now's the time! Hurry!"

With that, the old man turned away and disappeared into the bushes.

5

The next moment, James was running back toward the house as fast as he could go. He would do it all in the kitchen, he told himself—if only he could get in there without Aunt Sponge and Aunt Spiker seeing him. He was terribly excited. He flew through the long grass and the stinging-nettles, not caring whether he got stung or not on his bare knees, and in the distance he could see Aunt Sponge and Aunt Spiker sitting in their chairs with their backs toward him. He swerved away from them so as to go around the other side of the house, but then suddenly, just as he was passing underneath the old peach tree that stood in the middle of the garden, his foot slipped and he fell flat on his face in the grass. The paper bag burst open as it hit the ground and the thousands of tiny green things were scattered in all directions.

James immediately picked himself up onto his hands and knees and started searching around for his precious treasures. *But what was this?* They were all sinking into the soil! He could actually see them wriggling and twisting as they burrowed their way downward into the hard earth, and at once he reached out a hand to pick some of them up before it was too late, but they disappeared right under his fingers. He went after some others, and the same thing happened! He began scrabbling around frantically in an effort to catch hold of those that were left, but they were too quick for him. Each time the tips of his fingers were just about to touch them, they vanished into the earth! And soon, in the space of only a few seconds, every single one of them had gone!

James felt like crying. He would never get them back now—they were lost, lost, lost forever.

But where had they gone to? And why in the world had they been so eager to push down into the earth like that? What were they after? There was nothing down *there*. Nothing except the roots of the old peach tree…and a whole lot of earthworms and centipedes and insects living in the soil.

But what was it that the old man had said? *Whoever they meet first, be it bug, insect, animal, or tree, that will be the one who gets the full power of their magic!*

Good heavens, thought James. What is going to happen in that case if they *do* meet an earthworm? Or a centipede? Or a spider? And what if they *do* go into the roots of the peach tree?

"Get up at once, you lazy little beast!" a voice was suddenly shouting in James's ear. James glanced up and saw Aunt Spiker standing over him, grim and tall and bony, glaring at him through her steel-rimmed spectacles. "Get back over there immediately and finish chopping up those logs!" she ordered.

Aunt Sponge, fat and pulpy as a jellyfish, came waddling up behind her sister to see what was going on. "Why don't we just lower the boy down the well in a bucket and leave him there for the night?" she suggested. "That ought to teach him not to laze around like this the whole day long."

"That's a very good wheeze, my dear Sponge. But let's make him finish chopping up the wood first. Be off with you at once, you hideous brat, and do some work!"

Slowly, sadly, poor James got up off the ground and went back to the woodpile. Oh, if only he hadn't slipped and fallen and dropped that precious bag. All hope of a happier life had gone completely now. Today and tomorrow and the next day and all the other days as well would be nothing but punishment and pain, unhappiness and despair.

He picked up the chopper and was just about to start chopping away again when he heard a shout behind him that made him stop and turn.

6

"Sponge! Sponge! Come here at once and look at this!"

"At what?"

"It's a peach!" Aunt Spiker was shouting.

"A what?"

"A peach! Right up there on the highest branch! Can't you see it?"

"I think you must be mistaken, my dear Spiker. That miserable tree *never* has any peaches on it."

"There's one on it now, Sponge! You look for yourself!"

"You're teasing me, Spiker. You're making my mouth water

on purpose when there's nothing to put into it. Why, that tree's never even had a *blossom* on it, let alone a peach. Right up on the highest branch, you say? I can't see a thing. Very funny... Ha, ha...*Good gracious* me! Well, *I'll be blowed!* There really *is* a peach up there!"

"A nice big one, too!" Aunt Spiker said.

"A beauty, a beauty!" Aunt Sponge cried out.

At this point, James slowly put down his chopper and turned and looked across at the two women, who were standing underneath the peach tree.

Something is about to happen, he told himself. *Something peculiar is about to happen any moment.* He hadn't the faintest idea what it might be, but he could feel it in his bones that something was going to happen soon. He could feel it in the air around him...in the sudden stillness that had fallen upon the garden....

James tiptoed a little closer to the tree. The aunts were not talking now. They were just standing there, staring at the peach. There was not a sound anywhere, not even a breath of wind, and overhead the sun blazed down upon them out of a deep blue sky.

"It looks ripe to me," Aunt Spiker said, breaking the silence.

"Then why don't we eat it?" Aunt Sponge suggested, licking her thick lips. "We can have half each. Hey, you! James! Come over here at once and climb this tree!"

James came running over.

"I want you to pick that peach up there on the highest branch," Aunt Sponge went on. "Can you see it?"

"Yes, Auntie Sponge, I can see it!"

"And don't you dare to eat any of it yourself. Your Aunt Spiker and I are going to have it between us right here and now, half each. Get on with you! Up you go!"

James crossed over to the tree trunk.

"Stop!" Aunt Spiker said quickly. "Hold everything!" She was staring up into the branches with her mouth wide open and her eyes bulging as though she had seen a ghost. *"Look!"* she said. *"Look,* Sponge, *look!"*

"What's the matter with you?" Aunt Sponge demanded.

"It's *growing*!" Aunt Spiker cried. "It's getting bigger and bigger!"

"What is?"

"The peach, of course!"

"You're joking!"

"Well, look for yourself!"

"But my dear Spiker, that's perfectly ridiculous. That's impossible. That's—that's—that's—Now, wait *just* a minute—No—No—that can't be right—No—Yes—Great Scott! The thing really *is* growing!"

"It's nearly twice as big already!" Aunt Spiker shouted.

"It can't be true!"

"It *is* true!"

"It must be a miracle!"

"Watch it! Watch it!"

"I *am* watching it!"

"Great Heavens alive!" Aunt Spiker yelled. "I can actually see the thing bulging and swelling before my very eyes!"

7

The two women and the small boy stood absolutely still on the grass underneath the tree, gazing up at this extraordinary fruit. James's little face was glowing with excitement, his eyes were as big and bright as two stars. He could see the peach swelling larger and larger as clearly as if it were a balloon being blown up.

In half a minute, it was the size of a melon!

In another half-minute, it was *twice* as big again!

"Just *look* at it growing!" Aunt Spiker cried.

"Will it ever stop!" Aunt Sponge shouted, waving her fat arms and starting to dance around in circles.

And now it was so big it looked like an enormous butter-colored pumpkin dangling from the top of the tree.

"Get away from that tree trunk, you stupid boy!" Aunt Spiker yelled. "The slightest shake and I'm sure it'll fall off! It must weigh twenty or thirty pounds at least!"

The branch that the peach was growing upon was beginning to bend over further and further because of the weight.

"Stand back!" Aunt Sponge shouted. "It's coming down! The branch is going to break!"

But the branch didn't break. It simply bent over more and more as the peach got heavier and heavier.

And still it went on growing.

In another minute, this mammoth fruit was as large and round and fat as Aunt Sponge herself, and probably just as heavy.

"It *has* to stop now!" Aunt Spiker yelled. "It can't go on forever!"

But it didn't stop.

Soon it was the size of a small car, and reached halfway to the ground.

Both aunts were now hopping around and around the tree, clapping their hands and shouting all sorts of silly things in their excitement.

"Hallelujah!" Aunt Spiker shouted. "What a peach! What a peach!"

"Terrifico!" Aunt Sponge cried out, "Magnifico! Splendifico! And what a meal!"

"It's still growing!"

"I know! I know!"

As for James, he was so spellbound by the whole thing that he could only stand and stare and murmur quietly to himself, "Oh, isn't it beautiful. It's the most beautiful thing I've ever seen."

"Shut up, you little twerp!" Aunt Spiker snapped, happening to overhear him. "It's none of your business!"

"That's right," Aunt Sponge declared. "It's got nothing to do with you whatsoever! Keep out of it!"

"Look!" Aunt Spiker shouted. "It's growing faster than ever now! It's speeding up!"

"I see it, Spiker! I do! I do!"

Bigger and bigger grew the peach, bigger and bigger and bigger.

Then at last, when it had become

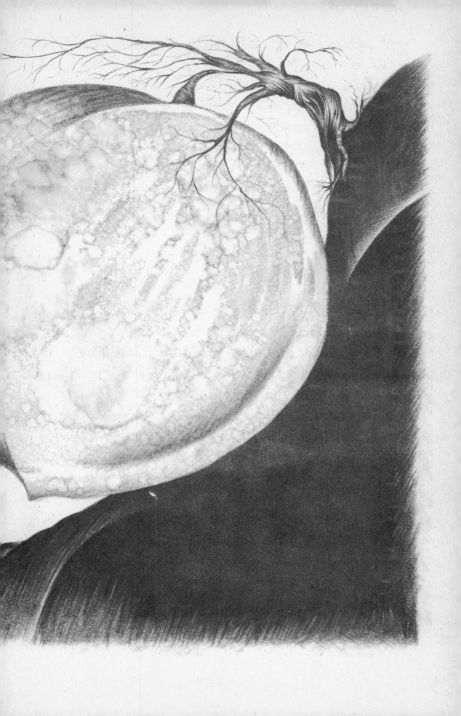

nearly as tall as the tree that it was growing on, as tall and wide, in fact, as a small house, the bottom part of it gently touched the ground—and there it rested.

"It can't fall off now!" Aunt Sponge shouted.

"It's stopped growing!" Aunt Spiker cried.

"No, it hasn't!"

"Yes, it has!"

"It's slowing down, Spiker, it's slowing down! But it hasn't stopped yet! You watch it!"

There was a pause.

"It has now!"

"I believe you're right."

"Do you think it's safe to touch it?"

"I don't know. We'd better be careful."

Aunt Sponge and Aunt Spiker began walking slowly around the peach, inspecting it very cautiously from all sides. They were like a couple of hunters who had just shot an elephant and were not quite sure whether it was dead or alive. And the massive round fruit towered over them so high that they looked like midgets from another world beside it.

The skin of the peach was very beautiful—a rich buttery yellow with patches of brilliant pink and red. Aunt Sponge advanced cautiously and touched it with the tip of one finger. "It's ripe!" she cried. "It's just perfect! Now, see here, Spiker. Why don't we go and get us a shovel right away and dig out a great big hunk of it for you and me to eat?"

"No," Aunt Spiker said. "Not yet."

"Whyever not?"

"Because I say so."

"But I can't *wait* to eat some!" Aunt Sponge cried out. She was watering at the mouth now and a thin trickle of spit was running down one side of her chin.

"My dear Sponge," Aunt Spiker said slowly, winking at her sister and smiling a sly, thin-lipped smile. "There's a pile of money to be made out of this if only we can handle it right. You wait and see."

8

The news that a peach almost as big as a house had suddenly appeared in someone's garden spread like wildfire across the countryside, and the next day a stream of people came scrambling up the steep hill to gaze upon this marvel.

Quickly, Aunt Sponge and Aunt Spiker called in carpenters and had them build a strong fence around the peach to save it from the crowd; and at the same time, these two crafty women stationed themselves at the front gate with a large bunch of tickets and started charging everyone for coming in.

"Roll up! Roll up!" Aunt Spiker yelled. "Only one shilling to see the giant peach!"

"Half price for children under six weeks old!" Aunt Sponge shouted.

"One at a time, please! Don't push! Don't push! You're all going to get in!"

"Hey, you! Come back, there! You haven't paid!"

By lunchtime, the whole place was a seething mass of men, women, and children all pushing and shoving to get a glimpse of this miraculous fruit. Helicopters were landing like wasps all over the hill, and out of them poured swarms of newspaper reporters, cameramen, and men from the television companies.

"It'll cost you double to bring in a camera!" Aunt Spiker shouted.

"All right! All right!" they answered. "We don't care!" And the money came rolling into the pockets of the two greedy aunts.

But while all this excitement was going on outside, poor James was forced to stay locked in his bedroom, peeping through the bars of his window at the crowds below.

"The disgusting little brute will only get in everyone's way if we let him wander about," Aunt Spiker had said early that morning.

"Oh, *please*!" he had begged. "I haven't met any other children for years and years and there are going to be lots of them down there for me to play with. And perhaps I could help you with the tickets."

"Cut it out!" Aunt Sponge had snapped. "Your Aunt Spiker and I are about to become millionaires, and the last thing we want is the likes of you messing things up and getting in the way."

Later, when the evening of the first day came and the people had all gone home, the aunts unlocked James's door and ordered him to go outside and pick up all the banana skins and orange peel and bits of paper that the crowd had left behind.

"Could I please have something to eat first?" he asked. "I haven't had a thing all day."

"No!" they shouted, kicking him out the door. "We're too busy to make food! We are counting our money!"

"But it's dark!" cried James.

"Get out!" they yelled. "And stay out until you've cleaned up all the mess!" The door slammed. The key turned in the lock.

9

Hungry and trembling, James stood alone out in the open, wondering what to do. The night was all around him now, and high overhead a wild white moon was riding in the sky. There was not a sound, not a movement anywhere.

Most people—and especially small children—are often quite scared of being out of doors alone in the moonlight. Everything is so deadly quiet, and the shadows are so long and black, and they keep turning into strange shapes that seem to move as you look at them, and the slightest little snap of a twig makes you jump.

James felt exactly like that now. He stared straight ahead with large frightened eyes, hardly daring to breathe. Not far away, in the middle of the garden, he could see the giant peach towering over everything else. Surely it was even bigger tonight than ever before? And what a dazzling sight it was! The moonlight was shining and glinting on its great curving sides, turning them to crystal and silver. It looked like a tremendous silver ball lying there in the grass, silent, mysterious, and wonderful.

And then all at once, little shivers of excitement started running over the skin on James's back.

Something else, he told himself, *something stranger than ever this time, is about to happen to me again soon.* He was sure of it. He could feel it coming.

He looked around him, wondering what on earth it was going to be. The garden lay soft and silver in the moonlight. The grass was wet with dew and a million dewdrops were sparkling and twinkling like diamonds around his feet. And now suddenly, the whole place, the whole garden, seemed to be *alive* with magic.

Almost without knowing what he was doing, as though drawn by some powerful magnet, James Henry Trotter started walking slowly toward the giant peach. He climbed over the fence that surrounded it, and stood directly beneath it, staring up at its great bulging sides. He put out a hand and touched it gently with the tip of one finger. It felt soft and warm and slightly furry, like the skin of a baby mouse. He moved a step closer and rubbed his cheek lightly against the soft skin. And then suddenly, while he was doing this, he happened to notice that right beside him and below him, close to the ground, there was a hole in the side of the peach.

10

It was quite a large hole, the sort of thing an animal about the size of a fox might have made.

James knelt down in front of it and poked his head and shoulders inside.

He crawled in.

He kept on crawling.

This isn't just a hole, he thought excitedly. *It's a tunnel!*

The tunnel was damp and murky, and all around him there

was the curious bittersweet smell of fresh peach. The floor was soggy under his knees, the walls were wet and sticky, and peach juice was dripping from the ceiling. James opened his mouth and caught some of it on his tongue. It tasted delicious.

He was crawling uphill now, as though the tunnel were leading straight toward the very center of the gigantic fruit. Every few seconds he paused and took a bite out of the wall. The peach flesh was sweet and juicy, and marvelously refreshing.

He crawled on for several more yards, and then suddenly— *bang*—the top of his head bumped into something extremely hard blocking his way. He glanced up. In front of him there was a solid wall that seemed at first as though it were made of wood. He touched it with his fingers. It certainly felt like wood, except that it was very jagged and full of deep grooves.

"Good heavens!" he said. "I know what this is! I've come to the stone in the middle of the peach!"

Then he noticed that there was a small door cut into the face of the peach stone. He gave a push. It swung open. He crawled through it, and before he had time to glance up

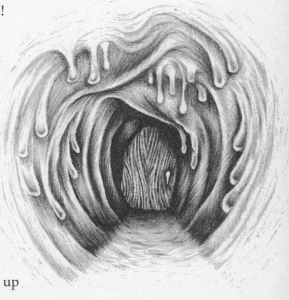

and see where he was, he heard a voice saying, "*Look* who's here!" And another one said, "We've been *waiting* for you!"

James stopped and stared at the speakers, his face white with horror.

He started to stand up, but his knees were shaking so much he had to sit down again on the floor. He glanced behind him, thinking he could bolt back into the tunnel the way he had come, but the doorway had disappeared. There was now only a solid brown wall behind him.

II

James's large frightened eyes traveled slowly around the room.

The creatures, some sitting on chairs, others reclining on a sofa, were all watching him intently.

Creatures?

Or were they insects?

An insect is usually something rather small, is it not? A grasshopper, for example, is an insect.

So what would you call it if you saw a grasshopper as large as a dog? As large as a *large* dog. You could hardly call *that* an insect, could you?

There was an Old-Green-Grasshopper as large as a large dog sitting on a stool directly across the room from James now.

And next to the Old-Green-Grasshopper, there was an enormous Spider.

And next to the Spider, there was a giant Ladybug with nine black spots on her scarlet shell.

Each of these three was squatting upon a magnificent chair.

On a sofa nearby, reclining comfortably in curled-up positions, there was a Centipede and an Earthworm.

On the floor over in the far corner, there was something thick and white that looked as though it might be a Silkworm. But it was sleeping soundly and nobody was paying any attention to it.

Every one of these "creatures" was at least as big as James himself, and in the strange greenish light that shone down from somewhere in the ceiling, they were absolutely terrifying to behold.

"I'm hungry!" the Spider announced suddenly, staring hard at James.

"*I'm* famished!" the Old-Green-Grasshopper said.

"So am *I*!" the Ladybug cried.

The Centipede sat up a little straighter on the sofa. "*Everyone's* famished!" he said. "We need food!"

Four pairs of round black glassy eyes were all fixed upon James.

The Centipede made a wriggling movement with his body as though he were about to glide off the sofa—but he didn't.

There was a long pause—and a long silence.

The Spider (who happened to be a female spider) opened her mouth and ran a long black tongue delicately over her lips. "Aren't *you* hungry?" she asked suddenly, leaning forward and addressing herself to James.

Poor James was backed up against the far wall, shivering with fright and much too terrified to answer.

"What's the matter with you?" the Old-Green-Grasshopper asked. "You look positively ill!"

"He looks as though he's going to faint any second," the Centipede said.

"Oh, my goodness, the poor thing!" the Ladybug cried. "I do believe he thinks it's *him* that we are wanting to eat!"

There was a roar of laughter from all sides.

"Oh dear, oh dear!" they said. "What an awful thought!"

"You mustn't be frightened," the Ladybug said kindly. "We wouldn't *dream* of hurting you. You are one of *us* now, didn't you know that? You are one of the crew. We're all in the same boat."

"We've been waiting for you all day long," the Old-Green-Grasshopper said. "We thought you were never going to turn up. I'm glad you made it."

"So cheer up, my boy, cheer up!" the Centipede said. "And meanwhile I wish you'd come over here and give me a hand with these boots. It takes me *hours* to get them all off by myself."

12

James decided that this was most certainly not a time to be disagreeable, so he crossed the room to where the Centipede was sitting and knelt down beside him.

"Thank you so much," the Centipede said. "You are very kind."

"You have a lot of boots," James murmured.

"I have a lot of legs," the Centipede answered proudly. "And a lot of feet. One hundred, to be exact."

"*There* he goes again!" the Earthworm cried, speaking for the first time. "He simply cannot stop telling lies about his legs! He doesn't have anything *like* a hundred of them! He's only got forty-two! The trouble is that most people don't bother to count them. They just take his word. And anyway, there is nothing *marvelous*, you know, Centipede, about having a lot of legs."

"Poor fellow," the Centipede said, whispering in James's ear. "He's blind. He can't see how splendid I look."

"In my opinion," the Earthworm said, "the *really* marvelous thing is to have no legs at all and to be able to walk just the same."

"You call that *walking*!" cried the Centipede. "You're a *slitherer*, that's all you are! You just *slither* along!"

"I glide," said the Earthworm primly.

"You are a slimy beast," answered the Centipede.

"I am *not* a slimy beast," the Earthworm said. "I am a useful and much loved creature. Ask any gardener you like. And as for you…"

"I am a pest!" the Centipede announced, grinning broadly and looking round the room for approval.

"He is *so* proud of that," the Ladybug said, smiling at James. "Though for the life of me I cannot understand why."

"I am the only pest in this room!" cried the Centipede, still grinning away. "Unless you count Old-Green-Grasshopper over there. But he is long past it now. He is too old to be a pest any more."

The Old-Green-Grasshopper turned his huge black eyes upon the Centipede and gave him a withering look. "Young fellow," he said, speaking in a deep, slow, scornful voice, "I have never been a pest in my life. I am a musician."

"Hear, hear!" said the Ladybug.

"James," the Centipede said. "Your names *is* James, isn't it?"

"Yes."

"Well, James, have you ever in your life seen such a marvelous colossal Centipede as me?"

"I certainly haven't," James answered. "How on earth did you get to be like that?"

"*Very* peculiar," the Centipede said. "*Very, very* peculiar indeed. Let me tell you what happened. I was messing about in the garden under the old peach tree and suddenly a funny little green thing came wriggling past my nose. Bright green it was, and extraordinarily beautiful, and it looked like some kind of a tiny stone or crystal…"

"Oh, but I know what that was!" cried James.

"It happened to me, too!" said the Ladybug.

"And me!" Miss Spider said. "Suddenly there were little green things everywhere! The soil was full of them!"

"I actually swallowed one!" the Earthworm declared proudly.

"So did I!" the Ladybug said.

"I swallowed three!" the Centipede cried. "But who's telling this story anyway? Don't interrupt!"

"It's too late to tell stories now," the Old-Green-Grasshopper announced. "It's time to go to sleep."

"I refuse to sleep in my boots!" the Centipede cried. "How many more are there to come off, James?"

"I think I've done about twenty so far," James told him.

"Then that leaves eighty to go," the Centipede said.

"*Twenty-two,* not *eighty*!" shrieked the Earthworm. "He's lying again."

The Centipede roared with laughter.

"Stop pulling the Earthworm's leg," the Ladybug said.

This sent the Centipede into hysterics. "Pulling his *leg*!" he cried, wriggling with glee and pointing at the Earthworm. "Which leg am I pulling? You tell me that?"

James decided that he rather liked the Centipede. He was obviously a rascal, but what a change it was to hear somebody laughing once in a while. He had never heard Aunt Sponge or Aunt Spiker laughing aloud in all the time he had been with them.

"We really *must* get some sleep," the Old-Green-Grasshopper said. "We've got a tough day ahead of us tomorrow. So would you be kind enough, Miss Spider, to make the beds?"

13

A few minutes later, Miss Spider had made the first bed. It was hanging from the ceiling, suspended by a rope of threads at either end so that actually it looked more like a hammock than a bed. But it was a magnificent affair, and the stuff that it was made of shimmered like silk in the pale light.

"I do hope you'll find it comfortable," Miss Spider said to the Old-Green-Grasshopper. "I made it as soft and silky as I possibly could. I spun it with gossamer. That's a much better quality thread than the one I use for my own web."

"Thank you so much, my dear lady," the Old-Green-Grasshopper said, climbing into the hammock. "Ah, this is just what I needed. Good night, everybody. Good night."

Then Miss Spider spun the next hammock, and the Ladybug got in.

After that, she spun a long one for the Centipede, and an even longer one for the Earthworm.

"And how do you like *your* bed?" she said to James when it came to his turn. "Hard or soft?"

"I like it soft, thank you very much," James answered.

"For goodness' sake stop staring round the room and get on with my boots!" the Centipede said. "You and I are never going to get any sleep at this rate! And kindly line them up neatly in pairs as you take them off. Don't just throw them over your shoulder."

James worked away frantically on the Centipede's boots. Each one had laces that had to be untied and loosened before it could be pulled off, and to make matters worse, all the laces were tied up in the most complicated knots that had to be unpicked with fingernails. It was just awful. It took about two hours. And by the time James had pulled off the last boot of all and had lined them up in a row on the floor—twenty-one pairs altogether—the Centipede was fast asleep.

"Wake up, Centipede," whispered James, giving him a gentle dig in the stomach. "It's time for bed."

"Thank you, my dear child," the Centipede said, opening his eyes. Then he got down off the sofa and ambled across the room and crawled into his hammock. James got into his own hammock—and oh, how soft and comfortable it was compared with the hard bare boards that his aunts had always made him sleep upon at home.

"Lights out," said the Centipede drowsily.

Nothing happened.

"Turn out the light!" he called, raising his voice.

James glanced round the room, wondering which of the others he might be talking to, but they were all asleep. The Old-Green-Grasshopper was snoring loudly through his nose. The Ladybug was making whistling noises as she breathed, and the Earthworm was coiled up like a spring at one end of his hammock, wheezing and blowing through his open mouth. As for Miss Spider, she had made a lovely web for herself across one corner of the room, and James could see her crouching right in the very center of it, mumbling softly in her dreams.

"I said turn out the light!" shouted the Centipede angrily.

"Are you talking to me?" James asked him.

"Of course I'm not talking to you, you ass!" the Centipede answered. "That crazy Glow-worm has gone to sleep with her light on!"

For the first time since entering the room, James glanced up at the ceiling—and there he saw a most extraordinary sight. Something that looked like a gigantic fly without wings (it was at least three feet long) was standing upside down upon its six legs in the middle of the ceiling, and the tail end of this creature seemed to be literally on fire. A brilliant greenish light as bright as the brightest electric bulb was shining out of its tail and lighting up the whole room.

"Is *that* a Glow-worm?" asked James, staring at the light. "It doesn't look like a worm of any sort to me."

"Of course it's a Glow-worm," the Centipede answered. "At least that's what *she* calls herself. Although actually you are quite right. She isn't really a worm at all. Glow-worms are never worms. They are simply lady fireflies without wings. Wake up, you lazy beast!"

But the Glow-worm didn't stir, so the Centipede reached out of his hammock and picked up one of his boots from the floor. "Put out that wretched light!" he shouted, hurling the boot up at the ceiling.

The Glow-worm slowly opened one eye and stared at the Centipede. "There is no need to be rude," she said coldly. "All in good time."

"Come on, come on, come on!" shouted the Centipede. "Or I'll put it out for you!"

"Oh, hello, James!" the Glow-worm said, looking down and giving James a little wave and a smile. "I didn't see you come in. Welcome, my dear boy, welcome—and good night!"

Then *click*—and out went the light.

James Henry Trotter lay there in the darkness with his eyes wide open, listening to the strange sleeping noises that the "creatures" were making all around him, and wondering what on earth was going to happen to him in the morning. Already, he was beginning to like his new friends very much. They were not nearly as terrible as they looked. In fact, they weren't really terrible at all. They seemed extremely kind and helpful in spite of all the shouting and arguing that went on between them.

"Good night, Old-Green-Grasshopper," he whispered. "Good night, Ladybug—Good night, Miss Spider—" But before he could go through them all, he had fallen fast asleep.

14

"We're off!" someone was shouting. "We're off at last!"

James woke up with a jump and looked about him. The creatures were all out of their hammocks and moving excitedly around the room. Suddenly the floor gave a great heave, as though an earthquake were taking place.

"Here we go!" shouted the Old-Green-Grasshopper, hopping up and down with excitement. "Hold on tight!"

"What's happening?" cried James, leaping out of his hammock. "What's going on?"

The Ladybug, who was obviously a kind and gentle creature, came over and stood beside him. "In case you don't know it," she said, "we are about to depart forever from the top of this ghastly hill that we've all been living on for so long. We are about to roll away inside this great big beautiful peach to a land of...of...of...to a land of—"

"Of what?" asked James.

"Never you mind," said the Ladybug. "But nothing could be worse than this desolate hilltop and those two repulsive aunts of yours—"

"Hear, hear!" they all shouted. "Hear, hear!"

"You may not have noticed it," the Ladybug went on, "but the whole garden, even before it reaches the steep edge of the hill, happens to be on a steep slope. And therefore the only thing that has been stopping this peach from rolling away right from the beginning is the thick stem attaching it to the tree. Break the stem, and off we go!"

"Watch it!" cried Miss Spider, as the room gave another violent lurch. "Here we go!"

"Not quite! Not quite!"

"At this moment," continued the Ladybug, "our Centipede, who has a pair of jaws as sharp as razors, is up there on top of the peach nibbling away at that stem. In fact, he must be nearly through it, as you can tell from the way we're lurching about. Would you like me to take you under my wing so that you won't fall over when we start rolling?"

"That's very kind of you," said James, "but I think I'll be all right."

Just then, the Centipede stuck his grinning face through a hole in the ceiling and shouted, "I've done it! We're off!"

"We're off!" the others cried. "We're off!"

"The journey begins!" shouted the Centipede.

"And who knows where it will end," muttered the Earthworm, "if *you* have anything to do with it. It can only mean trouble."

"Nonsense," said the Ladybug. "We are now about to visit the most marvelous places and see the most wonderful things! Isn't that so, Centipede?"

"There is no knowing what we shall see!" cried the Centipede.

"We may see a Creature with forty-nine heads
Who lives in the desolate snow,
And whenever he catches a cold (which he dreads)
He has forty-nine noses to blow.

"We may see the venomous Pink-Spotted Scrunch
Who can chew up a man with one bite.
It likes to eat five of them roasted for lunch
And eighteen for its supper at night.

"We may see a Dragon, and nobody knows
That we won't see a Unicorn there.
We may see a terrible Monster with toes
Growing out of the tufts of his hair.

"We may see the sweet little Biddy-Bright Hen
So playful, so kind and well-bred;
And such beautiful eggs! You just boil them and then
They explode and they blow off your head.

"A Gnu and a Gnocerous surely you'll see
And that gnormous and gnorrible Gnat
Whose sting when it stings you goes in at the knee
And comes out through the top of your hat.

"We may even get lost and be frozen by frost.
We may die in an earthquake or tremor.
Or nastier still, we may even be tossed
On the horns of a furious Dilemma.

"But who cares! Let us go from this horrible hill!
Let us roll! Let us bowl! Let us plunge!
Let's go rolling and bowling and spinning until
We're away from old Spiker and Sponge!"

One second later…slowly, insidiously, oh most gently, the great peach started to lean forward and steal into motion. The whole room began to tilt over and all the furniture went sliding across the floor, and crashed against the far wall. So did James and the Ladybug and the Old-Green-Grasshopper and Miss Spider and the Earthworm, also the Centipede, who had just come slithering quickly down the wall.

15

Outside in the garden, at that very moment, Aunt Sponge and Aunt Spiker had just taken their places at the front gate, each with a bunch of tickets in her hand, and the first stream of early-morning sightseers was visible in the distance climbing up the hill to view the peach.

"We shall make a fortune today," Aunt Spiker was saying. "Just look at all those people!"

"I wonder what became of that horrid little boy of ours last night," Aunt Sponge said. "He never did come back in, did he?"

"He probably fell down in the dark and broke his leg," Aunt Spiker said.

"Or his neck, maybe," Aunt Sponge said hopefully.

"Just *wait* till I get my hands on him," Aunt Spiker said, waving her cane. "He'll never want to stay out all night again by the time *I've* finished with him. Good gracious me! What's that awful noise?"

Both women swung around to look.

The noise, of course, had been caused by the giant peach crashing through the fence that surrounded it, and now, gathering speed every second, it came rolling across the garden toward the place where Aunt Sponge and Aunt Spiker were standing.

They gaped. They screamed. They started to run. They panicked. They both got in each other's way. They began pushing and jostling, and each of them was thinking only about saving herself. Aunt Sponge, the fat one, tripped over a box that she'd brought along to keep the money in, and fell flat on her face. Aunt Spiker immediately tripped over Aunt Sponge and came down on top of her. They both lay on the ground, fighting and clawing and yelling and struggling frantically to get up again, but before they could do this, the mighty peach was upon them.

There was a crunch.

And then there was silence.

The peach rolled on. And behind it, Aunt Sponge and Aunt Spiker lay ironed out upon the grass as flat and thin and lifeless as a couple of paper dolls cut out of a picture book.

16

And now the peach had broken out of the garden and was over the edge of the hill, rolling and bouncing down the steep slope at a terrific pace. Faster and faster and faster it went, and the crowds of people who were climbing up the hill suddenly caught sight of this terrible monster plunging down upon them and they screamed and scattered to right and left as it went hurtling by.

At the bottom of the hill it charged across the road, knocking over a telegraph pole and flattening two parked automobiles as it went by.

Then it rushed madly across about twenty fields, breaking down all the fences and hedges in its path. It went right through the middle of a herd of fine Jersey cows, and then through a flock of sheep, and then through a paddock full of horses, and then through a yard full of pigs, and soon the whole countryside was a seething mass of panic-stricken animals stampeding in all directions.

The peach was still going at a tremendous speed with no sign of slowing down, and about a mile farther on it came to a village.

Down the main street of the village it rolled, with people leaping frantically out of its path right and left, and at the end of the street it went crashing right through the wall of an enormous building and out the other side, leaving two gaping round holes in the brickwork.

This building happened to be a famous factory where they

made chocolate, and almost at once a great river of warm melted chocolate came pouring out of the holes in the factory wall. A minute later, this brown sticky mess was flowing through every street in the village, oozing under the doors of houses and into people's shops and gardens. Children were wading in it up to their knees, and some were even trying to swim in it, and all of them were sucking it into their mouths in great greedy gulps and shrieking with joy.

But the peach rushed on across the countryside—on and on and on, leaving a trail of destruction in its wake. Cowsheds, stables, pigsties, barns, bungalows, hayricks, anything that got in its way went toppling over like a nine-pin. An old man sitting quietly beside a stream had his fishing rod whisked out of his hands as it went dashing by, and a woman called Daisy Entwistle was standing so close to it as it passed that she had the skin taken off the tip of her long nose.

Would it ever stop?

Why should it? A round object will always keep on rolling as long as it is on a downhill slope, and in this case the land sloped downhill all the way until it reached the ocean—the same ocean that James had begged his aunts to be allowed to visit the day before.

Well, perhaps he was going to visit it now. The peach was rushing closer and closer to it every second, and closer also to the towering white cliffs that came first.

These cliffs are the most famous in the whole of England, and they are hundreds of feet high. Below them, the sea is deep and cold and hungry. Many ships have been swallowed up and lost forever on this part of the coast, and all the men who were in them as well. The peach was now only a hundred yards away from the cliff—now fifty—now twenty—now ten—now five—and when it reached the edge of the cliff it seemed to leap up into the sky and hang there suspended for a few seconds, still turning over and over in the air…

Then it began to fall…

Down…

Down…

Down…

Down…

Down…

SMACK! It hit the water with a colossal splash and sank like a stone.

But a few seconds later, up it came again, and this time, up it stayed, floating serenely upon the surface of the water.

17

At this moment, the scene inside the peach itself was one of indescribable chaos. James Henry Trotter was lying bruised and battered on the floor of the room amongst a tangled mass of Centipede and Earthworm and Spider and Ladybug and Glow-worm and Old-Green-Grasshopper. In the whole history of the world, no travelers had ever had a more terrible journey than these unfortunate creatures. It had started out well, with much laughing and shouting, and for the first few seconds, as the peach had begun to roll slowly forward, nobody had minded being tumbled about a little bit. And when it went *BUMP!* and the Centipede had shouted, "*That* was Aunt Sponge!" and then *BUMP!* again, and "*That* was Aunt Spiker!" there had been a tremendous burst of cheering all around.

But as soon as the peach rolled out of the garden and began to go down the steep hill, rushing and plunging and bounding madly downward, then the whole thing became a nightmare. James found himself being flung up against the ceiling, then back onto the floor, then sideways against the wall, then up onto the ceiling again, and up and down and back and forth and round and round, and at the same time all the other creatures were flying through the air in every direction, and so were the chairs and the sofa, not to mention the forty-two boots belonging to the Centipede. Everything and all of them were being rattled around like peas inside an enormous rattle that was being rattled by a mad giant who refused to stop. To make it worse, something went wrong with the Glow-worm's lighting system, and the room was in pitchy darkness. There were screams and yells and curses and cries of pain, and everything kept going round and round, and once James made a frantic grab at some thick bars sticking out from the wall only to find that they were a couple of the Centipede's legs. "Let go, you idiot!" shouted the Centipede, kicking himself free, and James was promptly flung across the room into the Old-Green-Grasshopper's horny lap. Twice he got tangled up in Miss Spider's legs (a horrid business), and toward the end, the poor Earthworm, who was cracking himself like a whip every time he flew through the air from one side of the room to the other, coiled himself around James's body in a panic and refused to unwind.

Oh, it was a frantic and terrible trip!

But it was all over now, and the room was suddenly very

still and quiet. Everybody was beginning slowly and painfully to disentangle himself from everybody else.

"Let's have some light!" shouted the Centipede.

"Yes!" they cried. "Light! Give us some light!"

"I'm *trying*," answered the poor Glow-worm. "I'm doing my best. Please be patient."

They all waited in silence.

Then a faint greenish light began to glimmer out of the Glow-worm's tail, and this gradually became stronger and stronger until it was anyway enough to see by.

"*Some great journey!*" the Centipede said, limping across the room.

"I shall *never* be the same again," murmured the Earthworm.

"Nor I," the Ladybug said. "It's taken *years* off my life."

"But my dear friends!" cried the Old-Green-Grasshopper, trying to be cheerful, "we are *there*!"

"Where?" they asked. "Where? Where is *there*?"

"I don't know," the Old-Green-Grasshopper said. "But I'll bet it's somewhere good."

"We are probably at the bottom of a coal mine," the Earthworm said gloomily. "We certainly went down and down and down very suddenly at the last moment. I felt it in my stomach. I still feel it."

"Perhaps we are in the middle of a beautiful country full of songs and music," the Old-Green-Grasshopper said.

"Or near the seashore," said James eagerly, "with lots of other children down on the sand for me to play with!"

"Pardon me," murmured the Ladybug, turning a trifle pale, "but am I wrong in thinking that we seem to be bobbing up and down?"

"*Bobbing* up and down!" they cried. "What on earth do you mean?"

"You're still giddy from the journey," the Old-Green-Grasshopper told her. "You'll get over it in a minute. Is everybody ready to go upstairs now and take a look around?"

"Yes, yes!" they chorused. "Come on! Let's go!"

"I *refuse* to show myself out of doors in my bare feet," the Centipede said. "I have to get my boots on again first."

"For heaven's sake, let's not go through all that nonsense again," the Earthworm said.

"Let's *all* lend the Centipede a hand and get it over with," the Ladybug said. "Come on."

So they did, all except Miss Spider, who set about weaving a long rope-ladder that would reach from the floor up to a hole in the ceiling. The Old-Green-Grasshopper had wisely said that they must not risk going out of the side entrance when they didn't know where they were, but must first of all go up onto the top of the peach and have a look around.

So half an hour later, when the rope-ladder had been finished and hung, and the forty-second boot had been laced neatly onto the Centipede's forty-second foot, they were all ready to go out. Amidst mounting excitement and shouts of "Here we go, boys! The Promised Land! I can't wait to see it!" the whole company climbed up the ladder one by one and disappeared into a dark soggy tunnel in the ceiling that went steeply, almost vertically upward.

18

A minute later, they were out in the open, standing on the very top of the peach, near the stem, blinking their eyes in the strong sunlight and peering nervously around.

"What happened?"

"Where are we?"

"But this is *impossible*!"

"Unbelievable!"

"Terrible!"

"I *told* you we were bobbing up and down," the Ladybug said.

"We're in the middle of the sea!" cried James.

And indeed they were. A strong current and a high wind

had carried the peach so quickly away from the shore that already the land was out of sight. All around them lay the vast black ocean, deep and hungry. Little waves were bibbling against the sides of the peach.

"But how did it happen?" they cried. "Where are the fields? Where are the woods? Where is England?" Nobody, not even James, could understand how in the world a thing like this could have come about.

"Ladies and gentlemen," the Old-Green-Grasshopper said, trying very hard to keep the fear and disappointment out of his voice, "I am afraid that we find ourselves in a rather awkward situation."

"Awkward!" cried the Earthworm. "My dear Old Grasshopper, we are finished! Every one of us is about to perish! I may be blind, you know, but that much I can see quite clearly!"

"Off with my boots!" shouted the Centipede. "I cannot swim with my boots on!"

"I can't swim at all!" cried the Ladybug.

"Nor can I," wailed the Glow-worm.

"Nor I!" said Miss Spider. "None of us three girls can swim a single stroke."

"But you won't *have* to swim," said James calmly. "We are floating beautifully. And sooner or later a ship is bound to come along and pick us up."

They all stared at him in amazement.

"Are you quite sure that we are not sinking?" the Ladybug asked.

"Of course I'm sure," answered James. "Go and look for yourselves."

They all ran over to the side of the peach and peered down at the water below.

"The boy is quite right," the Old-Green-Grasshopper said. "We are floating beautifully. Now we must all sit down and keep perfectly calm. Everything will be all right in the end."

"What absolute nonsense!" cried the Earthworm. "Nothing is ever all right in the end, and well you know it!"

"Poor Earthworm," the Ladybug said, whispering in James's ear. "He loves to make everything into a disaster. He hates to be happy. He is only happy when he is gloomy. Now isn't that odd? But then, I suppose just *being* an Earthworm is enough to make a person pretty gloomy, don't you agree?"

"If this peach is not going to sink," the Earthworm was saying, "and if we are not going to be drowned, then every one of us is going to *starve* to death instead. Do you realize that we haven't had a thing to eat since yesterday morning?"

"By golly, he's right!" cried the Centipede. "For once, Earthworm is right!"

"Of course I'm right," the Earthworm said. "And we're not likely to find anything around here either. We shall get thinner and thinner and thirstier and thirstier, and we shall all die a slow and grisly death from starvation. I am dying already. I am slowly shriveling up for want of food. Personally, I would rather drown."

"But good heavens, you must be *blind*!" said James.

"You know very well I'm blind," snapped the Earthworm. "There's no need to rub it in."

"I didn't mean that," said James quickly. "I'm sorry. But can't you *see* that—"

"See?" shouted the poor Earthworm. "How can I see if I am blind?"

James took a deep, slow breath. "Can't you *realize*," he said patiently, "that we have enough food here to last us for weeks and weeks?"

"Where?" they said. "Where?"

"Why, the peach, of course! Our whole ship is made of food!"

"Jumping Jehoshaphat!" they cried. "We never thought of that!"

"My dear James," said the Old-Green-Grasshopper, laying a front leg affectionately on James's shoulder, "I don't know *what* we'd do without you. You are so clever. Ladies and gentlemen—we are saved again!"

"We are most certainly not!" said the Earthworm. "You must be crazy! You can't eat the ship! It's the only thing that is keeping us up!"

"We shall starve if we don't!" said the Centipede.

"And we shall drown if we do!" cried the Earthworm.

"Oh dear, oh dear," said the Old-Green-Grasshopper. "Now we're worse off than before!"

"Couldn't we just eat a *little* bit of it?" asked Miss Spider. "I am so dreadfully hungry."

"You can eat all you want," James answered. "It would take us weeks and weeks to make any sort of a dent in this enormous peach. Surely you can see that?"

"Good heavens, he's right again!" cried the Old-Green-Grasshopper, clapping his hands. "It would take weeks and weeks! Of course it would! But let's not go making a lot of holes all over the deck. I think we'd better simply scoop it out of that tunnel over there—the one that we've just come up by."

"An excellent idea," said the Ladybug.

"What are you looking so worried about, Earthworm?" the Centipede asked. "What's the problem?"

"The problem is…" the Earthworm said, "the problem is…well, the problem is that there is no problem!"

Everyone burst out laughing. "Cheer up, Earthworm!" they said. "Come and eat!" And they all went over to the tunnel entrance and began scooping out great chunks of juicy, golden-colored peach flesh.

"Oh, marvelous!" said the Centipede, stuffing it into his mouth.

"*Dee*-licious!" said the Old-Green-Grasshopper.

"Just fabulous!" said the Glow-worm.

"Oh my!" said the Ladybug primly. "What a heavenly taste!" She looked up at James, and she smiled, and James smiled back at her. They sat down on the deck together, both of them chewing away happily. "You know, James," the Ladybug said, "up until this moment, I have never in my life tasted anything except those tiny little green flies that live on rosebushes. They have a perfectly delightful flavor. But this peach is even better."

"Isn't it glorious!" Miss Spider said, coming over to join them. "Personally, I had always thought that a big, juicy, caught-in-the-web bluebottle was the finest dinner in the world—until I tasted this."

"*What* a flavor!" the Centipede cried. "It's terrific!

There's nothing like it! There never has been! And I should know because I personally have tasted all the finest foods in the world!" Whereupon, the Centipede, with his mouth full of peach and with juice running down all over his chin, suddenly burst into song:

"I've eaten many strange and scrumptious dishes
　　　　in my time,
Like jellied gnats and dandyprats and earwigs
　　　　cooked in slime,
And mice with rice—they're really nice
When roasted in their prime.
(But don't forget to sprinkle them with just a pinch
　　　　of grime.)

"I've eaten fresh mudburgers by the greatest cooks
　　　　there are,
And scrambled dregs and stinkbugs' eggs
　　　　and hornets stewed in tar,
And pails of snails and lizards' tails,
And beetles by the jar.
(A beetle is improved by just a splash of vinegar.)

"I often eat boiled slobbages. They're grand when
　　　　served beside
Minced doodlebugs and curried slugs. And have
　　　　you ever tried
Mosquitoes' toes and wampfish roes
Most delicately fried?
(The only trouble is they disagree with my inside.)

"I'm mad for crispy wasp-stings on a piece of
          buttered toast,
And pickled spines of porcupines. And then a
          gorgeous roast
Of dragon's flesh, well hung, not fresh—
It costs a buck at most,
(And comes to you in barrels if you order it by post.)

"I crave the tasty tentacles of octopi for tea,
I like hot-dogs, I LOVE hot-frogs, and surely
          you'll agree
A plate of soil with engine oil's
A super recipe.
(I hardly need to mention that it's practically free.)

"For dinner on my birthday shall I tell you what I
          chose:
Hot noodles made from poodles on a slice of garden
          hose—
And a rather smelly jelly
Made of armadillo's toes.
(The jelly is delicious, but you have to hold your
          nose.)

"Now comes," the Centipede declared, "the burden
          of my speech:
These foods are rare beyond compare—some are right
          out of reach;
But there's no doubt I'd go without
A million plates of each
For one small mite,
One tiny bite
Of this FANTASTIC PEACH!"

Everybody was feeling happy now. The sun was shining brightly out of a soft blue sky and the day was calm. The giant peach, with the sunlight glinting on its side, was like a massive golden ball sailing upon a silver sea.

19

"Look!" cried the Centipede just as they were finishing their meal. "Look at that funny thin black thing gliding through the water over there!"

They all swung around to look.

"There are two of them," said Miss Spider.

"There are *lots* of them!" said the Ladybug.

"What are they?" asked the Earthworm, getting worried.

"They must be some kind of fish," said the Old-Green-Grasshopper. "Perhaps they have come along to say hello."

"They are sharks!" cried the Earthworm. "I'll bet you anything you like that they are sharks and they have come along to eat us up!"

"What absolute rot!" the Centipede said, but his voice seemed suddenly to have become a little shaky, and he wasn't laughing.

"I am *positive* they are sharks!" said the Earthworm. "I just *know* they are sharks!"

And so, in actual fact, did everybody else, but they were too frightened to admit it.

There was a short silence. They all peered down anxiously at the sharks, who were cruising slowly round and round the peach.

"Just assuming that they *are* sharks," the Centipede said, "there still can't possibly be any danger if we stay up here."

But even as he spoke, one of those thin black fins suddenly changed direction and came cutting swiftly through the water right up to the side of the peach itself. The shark paused and stared up at the company with small evil eyes.

"Go away!" they shouted. "Go away, you filthy beast!"

Slowly, almost lazily, the shark opened his mouth (which was big enough to have swallowed a perambulator) and made a lunge at the peach.

They all watched, aghast.

And now, as though at a signal from the leader, all the other sharks came swimming in toward the peach, and they clustered around it and began to attack it furiously. There must have been twenty or thirty of them at least, all pushing and fighting and lashing their tails and churning the water into a froth.

Panic and pandemonium broke out immediately on top of the peach.

"Oh, we are finished now!" cried Miss Spider, wringing her feet. "They will eat up the whole peach and then there'll be nothing left for us to stand on and they'll start on us!"

"She is right!" shouted the Ladybug. "We are lost forever!"

"Oh, I don't want to be eaten!" wailed the Earthworm. "But they will take me first of all because I am so fat and juicy and I have no bones!"

"Is there *nothing* we can do?" asked the Ladybug, appealing to James. "Surely *you* can think of a way out of this."

Suddenly they were all looking at James.

"Think!" begged Miss Spider. "*Think*, James, *think*!"

"Come on," said the Centipede. "Come on, James. There *must* be *something* we can do."

Their eyes waited upon him, tense, anxious, pathetically hopeful.

20

"There *is something* that I believe we might try," James Henry Trotter said slowly. "I'm not saying it'll work..."

"Tell us!" cried the Earthworm. "Tell us quick!"

"We'll try anything you say!" said the Centipede. "But hurry, hurry, hurry!"

"Be quiet and let the boy speak!" said the Ladybug. "Go on, James."

They all moved a little closer to him. There was a longish pause.

"Go *on*!" they cried frantically. "*Go on!*"

And all the time while they were waiting they could hear the sharks threshing around in the water below them. It was enough to make anyone frantic.

"Come on, James," the Ladybug said, coaxing him.

"I...I...I'm afraid it's no good after all," James murmured, shaking his head. "I'm terribly sorry. I forgot. We don't have any string. We'd need hundreds of yards of string to make this work."

"What sort of string?" asked the Old-Green-Grasshopper sharply.

"Any sort, just so long as it's strong."

"But my dear boy, that's exactly what we do have! We've got all you want!"

"How? Where?"

"The Silkworm!" cried the Old-Green-Grasshopper. "Didn't you ever notice the Silkworm? She's still downstairs! She never moves! She just lies there sleeping all day long, but we can easily wake her up and make her spin!"

"And what about me, may I ask?" said Miss Spider. "I can spin just as well as any Silkworm. What's more, *I* can spin patterns."

"Can you make enough between you?" asked James.

"As much as you want."

"And quickly?"

"Of course! Of course!"

"And would it be strong?"

"The strongest there is! It's as thick as your finger! But why? What are you going to do?"

"I'm going to lift this peach clear out of the water!" James announced firmly.

"You're mad!" cried the Earthworm.

"It's our only chance."

"The boy's crazy!"

"He's joking!"

"Go on, James," the Ladybug said gently. "How are you going to do it?"

"Skyhooks, I suppose," jeered the Centipede.

"Seagulls," James answered calmly. "The place is full of them. Look up there!"

They all looked up and saw a great mass of seagulls wheeling round and round in the sky.

"I'm going to take a long silk string," James went on, "and I'm going to loop one end of it around a seagull's neck. And then I'm going to tie the other end to the stem of the peach." He pointed to the peach stem, which was standing up like a short thick mast in the middle of the deck.

"Then I'm going to get another seagull and do the same thing again, then another and another—"

"Ridiculous!" they shouted.

"Absurd!"

"Poppycock!"

"Balderdash!"

"Madness!"

And the Old-Green-Grasshopper said, "How can a few seagulls lift an enormous thing like this up into the air, and all of us as well? It would take hundreds...thousands..."

"There is no shortage of seagulls," James answered. "Look for yourself. We'll probably need four hundred, five hundred, six hundred...maybe even a thousand...I don't know...I shall simply go on hooking them up to the stem until we have enough to lift us. They'll be bound to lift us in the end. It's like balloons. You give someone enough balloons to hold, I mean *really* enough, then up he goes. And a seagull has far more lifting power than a balloon. If only we have the *time* to do it. If only we are not sunk first by those awful sharks...."

"You're absolutely off your head!" said the Earthworm. "How on earth do you propose to get a loop of string around a seagull's neck? I suppose you're going to fly up there yourself and catch it!"

"The boy's dotty!" said the Centipede.

"Let him finish," said the Ladybug. "Go on, James. How *would* you do it?"

"With bait."

"Bait! What sort of bait?"

"With a worm, of course. Seagulls love worms, didn't you know that? And luckily for us, we have here the biggest, fattest, pinkest, juiciest Earthworm in the world."

"You can stop right there!" the Earthworm said sharply. "That's quite enough!"

"Go on," the others said, beginning to grow interested. "Go on!"

"The seagulls have already spotted him," James continued. "That's why there are so many of them circling around. But they daren't come down to get him while all the rest of us are standing here. So this is what—"

"Stop!" cried the Earthworm. "Stop, stop, stop! I won't have it! I refuse! I—I—I—I—"

"Be quiet!" said the Centipede. "Mind your own business!"

"I like that!"

"My dear Earthworm, you're going to be eaten anyway, so what difference does it make whether it's sharks or seagulls?"

"I won't do it!"

"Why don't we hear what the plan is first?" said the Old-Green-Grasshopper.

"I don't give a hoot what the plan is!" cried the Earthworm. "I am not going to be pecked to death by a bunch of seagulls!"

"You will be a martyr," said the Centipede. "I shall respect you for the rest of my life."

"So will I," said Miss Spider. "And your name will be in all the newspapers. Earthworm gives life to save friends…"

"But he won't *have* to give his life," James told them. "Now listen to me. This is what we'll do…"

21

"Why, it's absolutely brilliant!" cried the Old-Green-Grasshopper when James had explained his plan.

"The boy's a genius!" the Centipede announced. "Now I can keep my boots on after all."

"Oh, I shall be pecked to death!" wailed the poor Earthworm.

"Of course you won't."

"I will, I know I will! And I won't even be able to see them coming at me because I have no eyes!"

James went over and put an arm gently around the Earthworm's shoulders. "I won't let them *touch* you," he said. "I promise I won't. But we've *got* to hurry! Look down there!"

There were more sharks than ever now around the peach. The water was boiling with them. There must have been ninety or a hundred at least. And to the travelers up on top, it certainly seemed as though the peach were sinking lower and lower into the water.

"Action stations!" James shouted. "Jump to it! There's not a moment to lose!" He was the captain now, and everyone knew it. They would do whatever he told them.

"All hands below deck except Earthworm!" he ordered.

"Yes, yes!" they said eagerly as they scuttled into the tunnel entrance. "Come on! Let's hurry!"

"And you—Centipede!" James shouted. "Hop downstairs and get that Silkworm to work at once! Tell her to spin as she's never spun before! Our lives depend upon it! And the same applies to you, Miss Spider! Hurry on down! Start spinning!"

22

In a few minutes everything was ready.

It was very quiet now on the top of the peach. There was nobody in sight—nobody except the Earthworm.

One half of the Earthworm, looking like a great, thick, juicy, pink sausage, lay innocently in the sun for all the seagulls to see.

The other half of him was dangling down the tunnel.

James was crouching close beside the Earthworm in the tunnel entrance, just below the surface, waiting for the first seagull. He had a loop of silk string in his hands.

The Old-Green-Grasshopper and the Ladybug were further down the tunnel, holding on to the Earthworm's tail, ready to pull him quickly in out of danger as soon as James gave the word.

And far below, in the great hollow stone of the peach, the Glow-worm was lighting up the room so that the two spinners, the Silkworm and Miss Spider, could see what they were doing.

The Centipede was down there, too, exhorting them both frantically to greater efforts, and every now and again James could hear his voice coming up faintly from the depths, shouting, "Spin, Silkworm, spin, you great fat lazy brute! Faster, faster, or we'll throw you to the sharks!"

"Here comes the first seagull!" whispered James. "Keep still now, Earthworm. Keep still. The rest of you get ready to pull."

"Please don't let it spike me," begged the Earthworm.

"I won't, I won't. Ssshhh…"

Out of the corner of one eye, James watched the seagull as it came swooping down toward the Earthworm. And then suddenly it was so close that he could see its small black eyes and its curved beak, and the beak was open, ready to grab a nice piece of flesh out of the Earthworm's back.

"Pull!" shouted James.

The Old-Green-Grasshopper and the Ladybug gave the Earthworm's tail an enormous tug, and like magic the Earthworm disappeared into the tunnel. At the same time, up went James's hand and the seagull flew right into the loop of silk that he was holding out. The loop, which had been cleverly made, tightened just the right amount (but not too much) around its neck, and the seagull was captured.

"Hooray!" shouted the Old-Green-Grasshopper, peering out of the tunnel. "Well done, James!"

Up flew the seagull with James paying out the silk string as it went. He gave it about fifty yards and then tied the string to the stem of the peach.

"Next one!" he shouted, jumping back into the tunnel. "Up you get again, Earthworm! Bring up some more silk, Centipede!"

"Oh, I don't like this at all," wailed the Earthworm. "It only just missed me! I even felt the wind on my back as it went swishing past!"

"Ssshh!" whispered James. "Keep still! Here comes another one!"

So they did it again.

And again, and again, and again.

And the seagulls kept coming, and James caught them one after the other and tethered them to the peach stem.

"One hundred seagulls!" he shouted, wiping the sweat from his face.

"Keep going!" they cried. "Keep going, James!"

"Two hundred seagulls!"

"Three hundred seagulls!"

"Four hundred seagulls!"

The sharks, as though sensing that they were in danger of losing their prey, were hurling themselves at the peach more furiously than ever, and the peach was sinking lower and lower still in the water.

"Five hundred seagulls!" James shouted.

"Silkworm says she's running out of silk!" yelled the Centipede from below. "She says she can't keep it up much longer. Nor can Miss Spider!"

"Tell them they've *got* to!" James answered. "They can't stop now!"

"We're lifting!" somebody shouted.

"No, we're not!"

"I felt it!"

"Put on another seagull, quick!"

"Quiet, everybody! Quiet! Here's one coming now!"

This was the five hundred and first seagull, and the moment that James caught it and tethered it to the stem with all the others, the whole enormous peach suddenly started rising up slowly out of the water.

"Look out! Here we go! Hold on, boys!"

But then it stopped.

And there it hung.

It hovered and swayed, but it went no higher.

The bottom of it was just touching the water. It was like a delicately balanced scale that needed only the tiniest push to tip it one way or the other.

"One more will do it!" shouted the Old-Green-Grasshopper, looking out of the tunnel. "We're almost there!"

And now came the big moment. Quickly, the five hundred and second seagull was caught and harnessed to the peach stem...

And then suddenly...

But slowly...

Majestically...

Like some fabulous golden balloon...

With all the seagulls straining at the strings above...

The giant peach rose up dripping out of the water and began climbing toward the heavens.

23

In a flash, everybody was up on top.

"Oh, isn't it beautiful!" they cried.

"What a marvelous feeling!"

"Good-by, sharks!"

"Oh, boy, this is the way to travel!"

Miss Spider, who was literally squealing with excitement, grabbed the Centipede by the waist and the two of them started dancing around and around the peach stem together. The Earthworm stood up on his tail and did a sort of wriggle of joy all by himself. The Old-Green-Grasshopper kept hopping higher and higher in the air. The Ladybug rushed over and shook James warmly by the hand. The Glow-worm, who at the best of times was a very shy and silent creature, sat glowing with pleasure near the tunnel entrance. Even the Silkworm, looking white and thin and completely exhausted, came creeping out of the tunnel to watch this miraculous ascent.

Up and up they went, and soon they were as high as the top of a church steeple above the ocean.

"I'm a bit worried about the peach," James said to the others as soon as all the dancing and the shouting had stopped. "I wonder how much damage those sharks have done to it underneath. It's quite impossible to tell from up here."

"Why don't I go over the side and make an inspection?" Miss Spider said. "It'll be no trouble at all, I assure you." And without waiting for an answer, she quickly produced a length of silk thread and attached the end of it to the peach stem. "I'll be back in a jiffy," she said, and then she walked calmly over to the edge of the peach and jumped off, paying out the thread behind her as she fell.

The others crowded anxiously around the place where she had gone over.

"Wouldn't it be dreadful if the thread broke," the Ladybug said.

There was a rather long silence.

"Are you all right, Miss Spider?" shouted the Old-Green-Grasshopper.

"Yes, thank you!" her voice answered from below. "I'm coming up now!" And up she came, climbing foot over foot up the silk thread, and at the same time tucking the thread back cleverly into her body as she climbed past it.

"Is it *awful*?" they asked her. "Is it all eaten away? Are there great holes in it everywhere?"

Miss Spider clambered back onto the deck with a pleased but also rather puzzled look on her face. "You won't believe this," she said, "but actually there's hardly any damage down there at all! The peach is almost untouched! There are just a few tiny pieces out of it here and there, but nothing more."

"You must be mistaken," James told her.

"Of course she's mistaken!" the Centipede said.

"I promise you I'm not," Miss Spider answered.

"But there were hundreds of sharks around us!"

"They churned the water into a froth!"

"We saw their great mouths opening and shutting!"

"I don't care what you saw," Miss Spider answered. "They certainly didn't do much damage to the peach."

"Then why did we start sinking?" the Centipede asked.

"Perhaps we *didn't* start sinking," the Old-Green-Grasshopper suggested. "Perhaps we were all so frightened that we simply imagined it."

This, in point of fact, was closer to the truth than any of them knew. A shark, you see, has an extremely long sharp nose, and its mouth is set very awkwardly underneath its face and a long way back. This makes it more or less impossible for it to get its teeth into a vast smooth curving surface such as the side of a peach. Even if the creature turns onto its back it still can't do it, because the nose always gets in the way. If you have ever seen a small dog trying to get its teeth into an enormous ball, then you will be able to imagine roughly how it was with the sharks and the peach.

"It must have been some kind of magic," the Ladybug said. "The holes must have healed up by themselves."

"Oh, look! There's a ship below *us*!" shouted James.

Everybody rushed to the side and peered over. None of them had ever seen a ship before.

"It looks like a big one."

"It's got three funnels."

"You can even see the people on the decks!"

"Let's wave to them. Do you think they can see us?"

Neither James nor any of the others knew it, but the ship that was now passing beneath them was actually the Queen Mary sailing out of the English Channel on her way to America. And on the bridge of the Queen Mary, the astonished Captain was standing with a group of his officers, all of them gaping at the great round ball hovering overhead.

"I don't like it," the Captain said.

"Nor do I," said the First Officer.

"Do you think it's following us?" said the Second Officer.

"I tell you I don't like it," muttered the Captain.

"It could be dangerous," the First Officer said.

"That's it!" cried the Captain. "It's a secret weapon! Holy cats! Send a message to the Queen at once! The country must be warned! And give me my telescope."

The First Officer handed the telescope to the Captain. The Captain put it to his eye.

"There's birds everywhere!" he cried. "The whole sky is teeming with birds! What in the world are *they* doing? And wait! Wait a second! There are *people* on it! I can see them moving! There's a—a—do I have this darned thing focused right? It looks like a little boy in short trousers! Yes, I can distinctly see a little boy in short trousers standing up there! And there's a—there's a—there's a—a—a—a sort of *giant ladybug*!"

"Now just a minute, Captain!" the First Officer said.

"And a *colossal green grasshopper*!"

"Captain!" the First Officer said sharply. "Captain, please!"

"And a *mammoth spider*!"

"Oh dear, he's been at the whisky again," whispered the Second Officer.

"And an *enormous—a simply enormous centipede*!" screamed the Captain.

"Call the Ship's Doctor," the First Officer said. "Our Captain is not well."

A moment later, the great round ball disappeared into a cloud, and the people on the ship never saw it again.

24

But up on the peach itself, everyone was still happy and excited.

"I wonder where we'll finish up this time," the Earthworm said.

"Who cares?" they answered. "Seagulls always go back to the land sooner or later."

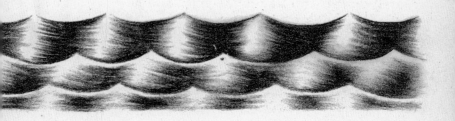

Up and up they went, high above the highest clouds, the peach swaying gently from side to side as it floated along.

"Wouldn't this be a perfect time for a little music?" the ladybug asked. "How about it, Old Grasshopper?"

"With pleasure, dear lady," the Old-Green-Grasshopper answered, bowing from the waist.

"Oh, hooray! He's going to play for us!" they cried, and immediately the whole company sat themselves down in a circle around the Old Green Musician—and the concert began.

From the moment that the first note was struck, the audience became completely spellbound. And as for James, never had he heard such beautiful music as this! In the garden at home on summer evenings, he had listened many times to the sound of grasshoppers chirping in the grass, and he had always liked the noise that they made. But this was a different kind of noise altogether. This was real music—chords, harmonies, tunes, and all the rest of it.

And what a wonderful instrument the Old-Green-Grasshopper was playing on. It was like a violin! It was almost exactly as though he were playing upon a violin!

The bow of the violin, the part that moved, was his back leg. The strings of the violin, the part that made the sound, was the edge of his wing.

He was using only the top of his back leg (the thigh), and he was stroking this up and down against the edge of his wing with incredible skill, sometimes slowly, sometimes fast, but always with the same easy flowing action. It was precisely the way a clever violinist would have used his bow; and the music came pouring out and filled the whole blue sky around them with magic melodies.

When the first part was finished, everyone clapped madly, and Miss Spider stood up and shouted, "Bravo! Encore! Give us some more!"

"Did you like that, James?" the Old-Green-Grasshopper asked, smiling at the small boy.

"Oh, I loved it!" James answered. "It was beautiful! It was as though you had a real violin in your hands!"

"A *real* violin!" the Old-Green-Grasshopper cried. "Good heavens, I like that! My dear boy, I *am* a real violin! It is part of my own body!"

"But do *all* grasshoppers play their music on violins, the same way as you do?" James asked him.

"No," he answered, "not all. If you want to know, I happen to be a 'short-horned' grasshopper. I have two short feelers coming out of my head. Can you see them? There they are. They are quite short, aren't they? That's why they call me a 'short-horn.' And we 'short-horns' are the only ones who play our music in the violin style, using a bow. My 'long-horned' relatives, the ones who have long curvy feelers coming out of their heads, make their music simply by rubbing the edges of their two top wings together. They are not violinists, they are wing-rubbers. And a rather inferior noise these wing-rubbers produce, too, if I may say so. It sounds more like a banjo than a fiddle."

"How fascinating this all is!" cried James. "And to think that up until now I had never even *wondered* how a grass-hopper made his sounds."

"My dear young fellow," the Old-Green-Grasshopper said gently, "there are a whole lot of things in this world of ours that you haven't started wondering about yet. Where, for example, do you think that I keep my ears?"

"Your ears? Why, in your head, of course."

Everyone burst out laughing.

"You mean you don't even know *that*?" cried the Centipede.

"Try again," said the Old-Green-Grasshopper, smiling at James.

"You can't possibly keep them anywhere else?"

"Oh, can't I?"

"Well—I give up. Where *do* you keep them?"

"Right here," the Old-Green-Grasshopper said. "One on each side of my tummy."

"It's not true!"

"Of course it's true. What's so peculiar about that? You ought to see where my cousins the crickets and the katydids keep theirs."

"Where do they keep them?"

"In their legs. One in each front leg, just below the knee."

"You mean you didn't know that either?" the Centipede said scornfully.

"You're joking," James said. "Nobody could possibly have his ears in his legs."

"Why not?"

"Because...because it's ridiculous, that's why."

"You know what I think is ridiculous?" the Centipede said, grinning away as usual. "I don't mean to be rude, but *I* think it is ridiculous to have ears on the sides of one's head. It certainly *looks* ridiculous. You ought to take a peek in the mirror some day and see for yourself."

"Pest!" cried the Earthworm. "Why must you always be so rude and rambunctious to everyone? You ought to apologize to James at once."

25

James didn't want the Earthworm and the Centipede to get into another argument, so he said quickly to the Earthworm, "Tell me, do *you* play any kind of music?"

"No, but I do *other* things, some of which are really quite *extraordinary*," the Earthworm said, brightening.

"Such as what?" asked James.

"Well," the Earthworm said. "Next time you stand in a field or in a garden and look around you, then just remember this: that every grain of soil upon the surface of the land, every tiny little bit of soil that you can see, has actually passed through the body of an Earthworm during the last few years! Isn't that wonderful?"

"It's not possible!" said James.

"My dear boy, it's a fact."

"You mean you actually *swallow* soil?"

"Like mad," the Earthworm said proudly. "*In* one end and *out* the other."

"But what's the point?"

"What do you mean, what's the point?"

"Why do you do it?"

"We do it for the farmers. It makes the soil nice and light and crumbly so that things will grow well in it. If you really want to know, the farmers couldn't do without us. We are essential. We are vital. So it is only natural that the farmer should love us. He loves us even more, I believe, than he loves the Ladybug."

"The Ladybug!" said James, turning to look at her. "Do they love you, too?"

"I am told that they do," the Ladybug answered modestly, blushing all over. "In fact, I understand that in some places the farmers love us so much that they go out and buy live Ladybugs by the sackful and take them home and set them free in their fields. They are very pleased when they have lots of Ladybugs in their fields."

"But why?" James asked.

"Because we gobble up all the nasty little insects that are gobbling up all the farmer's crops. It helps enormously, and we ourselves don't charge a penny for our services."

"I think you're wonderful," James told her. "Can I ask you one special question?"

"Please do."

"Well, is it really true that I can tell how old a Ladybug is by counting her spots?"

"Oh no, that's just a children's story," the Ladybug said. "We never change our spots. Some of us, of course, are born with more spots than others, but we never change them. The number of spots that a Ladybug has is simply a way of showing which branch of the family she belongs to. I, for example, as you can see for yourself, am a Nine-Spotted Ladybug. I am very lucky. It is a fine thing to be."

"It is, indeed," said James, gazing at the beautiful scarlet shell with the nine black spots on it.

"On the other hand," the Ladybug went on, "some of my less fortunate relatives have no more than two spots altogether on their shells! Can you imagine that? They are called Two-Spotted Ladybugs, and very common and ill-mannered they are, I regret to say. And then, of course, you have the Five-Spotted Ladybugs as well. They are much nicer than the Two-Spotted ones, although I myself find them a trifle too saucy for my taste."

"But they are all of them loved?" said James.

"Yes," the Ladybug answered quietly. "They are all of them loved."

"It seems that almost *everyone* around here is loved!" said James. "How nice this is!"

"Not me!" cried the Centipede happily. "I am a pest and I'm proud of it! Oh, I am such a shocking dreadful pest!"

"Hear, hear," the Earthworm said.

"But what about you, Miss Spider?" asked James. "Aren't you also much loved in the world?"

"Alas, no," Miss Spider answered, sighing long and loud. "I am not loved at all. And yet I do nothing but good. All day long I catch flies and mosquitoes in my webs. I am a decent person."

"I know you are," said James.

"It is very unfair the way we Spiders are treated," Miss Spider went on. "Why, only last week your own horrible Aunt Sponge flushed my poor dear father down the plug-hole in the bathtub."

"Oh, how awful!" cried James.

"I watched the whole thing from a corner up in the ceiling," Miss Spider murmured. "It was ghastly. We never saw him again." A large tear rolled down her cheek and fell with a splash on the floor.

"But is it not very unlucky to kill a spider?" James inquired, looking around at the others.

"Of course it's unlucky to kill a spider!" shouted the Centipede. "It's about the unluckiest thing anyone can do. Look what happened to Aunt Sponge after she'd done that! *Bump!* We all felt it, didn't we, as the peach went over her? Oh, what a lovely bump that must have been for you, Miss Spider!"

"It was very satisfactory," Miss Spider answered. "Will you sing us a song about it, please?"

So the Centipede did.

> *"Aunt Sponge was terrifically fat,*
> *And tremendously flabby at that.*
> *Her tummy and waist*
> *Were as soggy as paste—*
> *It was worse on the place where she sat!*

So she said, 'I must make myself flat.
I must make myself sleek as a cat.
I shall do without dinner
To make myself thinner.'
But along came the peach!
Oh, the beautiful peach!
And made her far thinner than that!"

"That was very nice," Miss Spider said. "Now sing one about Aunt Spiker."

"With pleasure," the Centipede answered, grinning:

"Aunt Spiker was thin as a wire,
And as dry as a bone, only drier.
She was so long and thin
If you carried her in
You could use her for poking the fire!

'I must do something quickly,' she frowned.
'I want FAT. I want pound upon pound!
I must eat lots and lots
Of marshmallows and chocs
Till I start bulging out all around.'

'Ah, yes,' she announced, 'I have sworn
That I'll alter my figure by dawn!'
Cried the peach with a snigger,
'I'LL alter your figure—'
And ironed her out on the lawn!"

Everybody clapped and called out for more songs from the Centipede, who at once launched into his favorite song of all:

"Once upon a time
When pigs were swine
And monkeys chewed tobacco
And hens took snuff
To make themselves tough
And the ducks said quack-quack-quacko,
And porcupines
Drank fiery wines
And goats ate tapioca
And Old Mother Hubbard
Got stuck in the c—"

"Look out, Centipede!" cried James. "Look out!"

26

The Centipede, who had begun dancing wildly around the deck during the song, had suddenly gone too close to the downward curving edge of the peach, and for three awful seconds he had stood teetering on the brink, swinging his legs frantically in circles in an effort to stop himself from falling over backward into space. But before anyone could reach him—down he went! He gave a shriek of terror as he fell, and the others, rushing to the side and peering over, saw his poor long body tumbling over and over through the air, getting smaller and smaller until it was out of sight.

"Silkworm!" yelled James. "Quick! Start spinning!"

The Silkworm sighed, for she was still very tired from spinning all that silk for the seagulls, but she did as she was told.

"I'm going down after him!" cried James, grabbing the silk string as it started coming out of the Silkworm and tying the end of it around his waist. "The rest of you hold on to Silkworm so I don't pull her over with me, and later on, if you feel three tugs on the string, start hauling me up again!"

He jumped, and he went tumbling down after the Centipede, down, down, down, toward the sea below, and you can imagine how quickly the Silkworm had to spin to keep up with the speed of his fall.

"We'll never see either of them again!" cried the Ladybug. "Oh, dear! Oh, dear! Just when we were all so happy, too!"

Miss Spider, the Glow-worm, and the Ladybug all began to cry. So did the Earthworm. "I don't care a bit about the Centipede," the Earthworm sobbed. "But I really did love that little boy."

Very softly, the Old-Green-Grasshopper started to play the Funeral March on his violin, and by the time he had finished, everyone, including himself, was in a flood of tears.

Suddenly, there came three sharp tugs on the rope. "Pull!" shouted the Old-Green-Grasshopper. "Everyone get behind me and pull!"

There was about a mile of string to be hauled in, but they all worked like mad, and in the end, over the side of the peach, there appeared a dripping-wet James with a dripping-wet Centipede clinging to him tightly with all forty-two of his legs.

"He saved me!" gasped the Centipede. "He swam around in the middle of the Atlantic Ocean until he found me!"

"My dear boy," the Old-Green-Grasshopper said, patting James on the back. "I do congratulate you."

"My boots!" cried the Centipede. "Just look at my precious boots! They are ruined by the water!"

"Be quiet!" the Earthworm said. "You are lucky to be alive."

"Are we still going up and up?" asked James.

"We certainly are," answered the Old-Green-Grasshopper. "And it's beginning to get dark."

"I know. It'll soon be night."

"Why don't we all go down below and keep warm until tomorrow morning?" Miss Spider suggested.

"No," the Old-Green-Grasshopper said. "I think that would be very unwise. It will be safer if we all stay up here through the night and keep watch. Then, if anything happens, we shall anyway be ready for it."

27

James Henry Trotter and his companions crouched close together on top of the peach as the night began closing in around them. Clouds like mountains towered high above their heads on all sides, mysterious, menacing, overwhelming. Gradually it grew darker and darker, and then a pale three-quarter moon came up over the tops of the clouds and cast an eerie light over the whole scene. The giant peach swayed gently from side to side as it floated along, and the hundreds of silky white strings going upward from its stem were beautiful in the moonlight. So also was the great flock of seagulls overhead.

There was not a sound anywhere. Traveling upon the peach was not in the least like traveling in an airplane. The airplane comes clattering and roaring through the sky, and whatever might be lurking secretly up there in the great cloud-mountains goes running for cover at its approach. That is why people who travel in airplanes never see anything.

But the peach…ah, yes…the peach was a soft, stealthy traveler, making no noise at all as it floated along. And several times during that long silent night ride high up over the middle of the ocean in the moonlight, James and his friends saw things that no one had ever seen before.

Once, as they drifted silently past a massive white cloud, they saw on the top of it a group of strange, tall, wispy-looking things that were about twice the height of ordinary men. They were not easy to see at first because they were almost as white as the cloud itself, but as the peach sailed closer, it became obvious that these "things" were actually living creatures—tall, wispy, wraithlike, shadowy white creatures who looked as though they were made out of a mixture of cotton-wool and candyfloss and thin white hairs.

"Ooooooooooooooh!" the Ladybug said. "I don't like this at all!"

"Ssshh!" James whispered back. "Don't let them hear you! They must be Cloud-Men!"

"*Cloud-Men!*" they murmured, huddling closer together for comfort. "Oh dear, oh dear!"

"I'm glad I'm blind and can't see them," the Earthworm said, "or I would probably scream."

"I hope they don't turn around and see *us*," Miss Spider stammered.

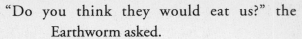

"Do you think they would eat us?" the Earthworm asked.

"They would eat *you*," the Centipede answered, grinning. "They would cut you up like a salami and eat you in thin slices."

The poor Earthworm began to quiver all over with fright.

"But what are they *doing*?" the Old-Green-Grasshopper whispered.

"I don't know," James answered softly. "Let's watch and see."

The Cloud-Men were all standing in a group, and they were doing something peculiar with their hands. First, they would reach out (all of them at once) and grab handfuls of cloud. Then they would roll these handfuls of cloud in their fingers until they turned into what looked like large white marbles. Then they would toss the marbles to one side and quickly grab more bits of cloud and start over again.

It was all very silent and mysterious. The pile of marbles beside them kept growing larger and larger. Soon there was a truckload of them there at least.

"They must be absolutely mad!" the Centipede said. "There's nothing to be afraid of here!"

"Be quiet, you pest!" the Earthworm whispered. "We shall all be eaten if they see us!"

But the Cloud-Men were much too busy with what they were doing to have noticed the great peach floating silently up behind them.

Then the watchers on the peach saw one of the Cloud-Men raising his long wispy arms above his head and they heard him shouting, "All right, boys! That's enough! Get the shovels!" And all the other Cloud-Men immediately let out a strange high-pitched whoop of joy and started jumping up and down and waving their arms in the air. Then they picked up enormous shovels and rushed over to the pile of marbles and began shoveling them as fast as they could over the side of the cloud, into space. *"Down they go!"* they chanted as they worked.

> *"Down they go!*
> *Hail and snow!*
> *Freezes and sneezes and noses will blow!"*

"It's *hailstones!*" whispered James excitedly. "They've been making hailstones and now they are showering them down onto the people in the world below!"

"Hailstones?" the Centipede said. "That's ridiculous! This is summertime. You don't have hailstones in summertime."

"They are practicing for the winter," James told him.

"I don't believe it!" shouted the Centipede, raising his voice.

"Ssshh!" the others whispered. And James said softly, "For heaven's sake, Centipede, don't make so much noise."

The Centipede roared with laughter. "Those imbeciles couldn't hear anything!" he cried. "They're deaf as doorknobs! You watch!" And before anyone could stop him, he had cupped his front feet to his mouth and was yelling at the Cloud-Men as loud as he could. "Idiots!" he yelled. "Nincompoops! Half-wits! Blunderheads! Asses! What on earth do you think you're doing over there!"

The effect was immediate. The Cloud-Men jumped around as if they had been stung by wasps. And when they saw the great golden peach floating past them not fifty yards away in the sky, they gave a yelp of surprise and dropped their shovels to the ground. And there they stood with the moonlight streaming down all over them, absolutely motionless, like a group of tall white hairy statues, staring and staring at the gigantic fruit as it went sailing by.

The passengers on the peach (all except the Centipede) sat frozen with terror, looking back at the Cloud-Men and wondering what was going to happen next.

"Now you've done it, you loathsome pest!" whispered the Earthworm to the Centipede.

"I'm not frightened of *them*!" shouted the Centipede, and to show everybody once again that he wasn't, he stood up to his full height and started dancing about and making insulting signs at the Cloud-Men with all forty-two of his legs.

This evidently infuriated the Cloud-Men beyond belief. All at once, they spun around and grabbed great handfuls of hailstones and rushed to the edge of the cloud and started throwing them at the peach, shrieking with fury all the time.

"Look out!" cried James. "Quick! Lie down! Lie flat on the deck!"

It was lucky they did! A large hailstone can hurt you as much as a rock or a lump of lead if it is thrown hard enough— and my goodness, how those Cloud-Men could throw! The hailstones came whizzing through the air like bullets from a machine gun, and James could hear them smashing against the sides of the peach and burying themselves in the peach flesh with horrible squelching noises—*plop! plop! plop! plop!* And then *ping! ping! ping!* as they bounced off the poor Ladybug's shell because she couldn't lie as flat as the others. And then

crack! as one of them hit the Centipede right on the nose and *crack!* again as another one hit him somewhere else.

"Ow!" he cried. "Ow! Stop! Stop! Stop!"

But the Cloud-Men had no intention of stopping. James could see them rushing about on the cloud like a lot of huge hairy ghosts, picking up hailstones from the pile, dashing to the edge of the cloud, hurling the hailstones at the peach, dashing back again to get more, and then, when the pile of stones was all gone, they simply grabbed handfuls of cloud and made as many more as they wanted, and much bigger ones now, some of them as large as cannon balls.

"Quickly!" cried James. "Down the tunnel or we'll all be wiped out!"

There was a rush for the tunnel entrance, and half a minute later everybody was safely downstairs inside the stone of the peach, trembling with fright and listening to the noise of the hailstones as they came crashing against the side of the peach.

"I'm a wreck!" groaned the Centipede. "I am wounded all over!"

"It serves you right," said the Earthworm.

"Would somebody kindly look and see if my shell is cracked?" the Ladybug said.

"Give us some light!" shouted the Old-Green-Grasshopper.

"I can't!" wailed the Glow-worm. "They've broken my bulb!"

"Then put in another one!" the Centipede said.

"Be quiet a moment," said James. "Listen! I do believe they're not hitting us any more!"

They all stopped talking and listened. Yes—the noise had ceased! The hailstones were no longer smashing against the peach.

"We've left them behind!"

"The seagulls must have pulled us away out of danger!"

"Hooray! Let's go up and see!"

Cautiously, with James going first, they all climbed back up the tunnel. James poked his head out and looked around. "It's all clear!" he called. "I can't see them anywhere!"

28

One by one, the travelers came out again onto the top of the peach and gazed carefully around. The moon was still shining as brightly as ever, and there were still plenty of huge shimmering cloud-mountains on all sides. But there were no Cloud-Men in sight now.

"The peach is leaking!" shouted the Old-Green-Grasshopper, peering over the side. "It's full of holes and the juice is dripping out everywhere!"

"*That* does it!" cried the Earthworm. "If the peach is leaking then we shall surely sink!"

"Don't be an ass!" the Centipede told him. "We're not in the water now!"

"Oh, look!" shouted the Ladybug. "Look, look, look! Over there!"

Everybody swung round to look.

In the distance and directly ahead of them, they now saw a most extraordinary sight. It was a kind of arch, a colossal curvy-shaped thing that reached high up into the sky and came down again at both ends. The ends were resting upon a huge flat cloud that was as big as a desert.

"Now what in the world is that?" asked James.

"It's a bridge!"

"It's an enormous hoop cut in half!"

"It's a giant horseshoe standing upside down!"

"Stop me if I'm wrong," murmured the Centipede, going white in the face, "but might those not be Cloud-Men climbing all over it?"

There was a dreadful silence. The peach floated closer and closer.

"They *are* Cloud-Men!"

"There are hundreds of them!"

"Thousands!"

"Millions!"

"I don't want to hear about it!" shrieked the poor blind Earthworm. "I'd rather be on the end of a fish hook and used as bait than come up against those terrible creatures again!"

"I'd rather be fried alive and eaten by a Mexican!" wailed the Old-Green-Grasshopper.

"Please keep quiet," whispered James. "It's our only hope."

They crouched very still on top of the peach, staring at the Cloud-Men. The whole surface of the cloud was literally *swarming* with them, and there were hundreds more up above, climbing about on that monstrous crazy arch.

"But what *is* that thing?" whispered the Ladybug. "And what are they *doing* to it?"

"I don't care what they're doing to it!" the Centipede said, scuttling over to the tunnel entrance. "I'm not staying up here! Good-by!"

But the rest of them were too frightened or too hypnotized by the whole affair to make a move.

"Do you know what?" James whispered.

"*What?*" they said. "*What?*"

"That enormous arch—they seem to be *painting* it! They've got pots of paint and big brushes! You look!"

And he was quite right. The travelers were close enough now to see that this was exactly what the Cloud-Men were doing. They all had huge brushes in their hands and they were splashing the paint onto the great curvy arch in a frenzy of speed, so fast, in fact, that in a few minutes the whole of the arch became covered with the most glorious colors—reds, blues, greens, yellows, and purples.

"It's a rainbow!" everyone said at once. "They are making a rainbow!"

"Oh, isn't it beautiful!"

"Just look at those colors!"

"Centipede!" they shouted. "You *must* come up and see this!" They were so enthralled by the beauty and brilliance of the rainbow that they forgot to keep their voices low any longer. The Centipede poked his head cautiously out of the tunnel entrance.

"Well well well," he said. "I've *always* wondered how those things were made. But why all the ropes? What are they doing with those ropes?"

"Good heavens, they are pushing it off the cloud!" cried James. "There it goes! They are lowering it down to the earth with ropes!"

"And I'll tell you something else," the Centipede said sharply. "If I'm not greatly mistaken, we ourselves are going to bump right into it!"

"Bless my soul, he's right!" the Old-Green-Grasshopper exclaimed.

The rainbow was now dangling in the air below the cloud. The peach was also just below the level of the cloud, and it was heading directly toward the rainbow, traveling rather fast.

"We are lost!" Miss Spider cried, wringing her feet again. "The end has come!"

"I can't stand it!" wailed the Earthworm. "Tell me what's happening!"

"We're going to miss it!" shouted the Ladybug.

"No, we're not!"

"Yes, we are!"

"Yes!—Yes!—No!—Oh, my heavens!"

"Hold on, everybody!" James called out, and suddenly there was a tremendous thud as the peach went crashing into the top part of the rainbow. This was followed by an awful splintering noise as the enormous rainbow snapped right across the middle and became two separate pieces.

The next thing that happened was extremely unfortunate. The ropes that the Cloud-Men had been using for lowering the rainbow got tangled up with the silk strings that went up from the peach to the seagulls! The peach was trapped! Panic and pandemonium broke out among the travelers, and James Henry Trotter, glancing up quickly, saw the faces of a thousand furious Cloud-Men peering down at him over the edge of the cloud. The faces had almost no shape at all because of the long white hairs that covered them. There were no noses, no mouths, no ears, no chins—only the eyes were visible in each face, two small black eyes glinting malevolently through the hairs.

Then came the most frightening thing of all. One Cloud-Man, a huge hairy creature who must have been fourteen feet tall at least, suddenly stood up and made a tremendous leap off the side of the cloud, trying to get to one of the silk strings above the peach. James and his friends saw him go flying through the air above them, his arms outstretched in front of him, reaching for the nearest string, and they saw him grab it and cling to it with his hands and legs. And then, very very slowly, hand over hand, he began to come down the string.

"Mercy! Help! Save us!" cried the Ladybug.

"He's coming down to eat us!" wailed the Old-Green-Grasshopper. "Jump overboard!"

"Then eat the Earthworm first!" shouted the Centipede. "It's no good eating me, I'm full of bones like a kipper!"

"Centipede!" yelled James. "Quickly! Bite through that string, the one he's coming down on!"

The Centipede rushed over to the stem of the peach and took the silk string in his teeth and bit through it with one snap of his jaws. Immediately, far above them, a single seagull was seen to come away from the rest of the flock and go flying off with a long string trailing from its neck. And clinging desperately to the end of the string, shouting and cursing with fury, was the huge hairy Cloud-Man. Up and up he went, swinging across the moonlit sky, and James Henry Trotter, watching him with delight, said, "My goodness, he must weigh almost nothing at all for one seagull to be able to pull him up like that! He must be all hair and air!"

The rest of the Cloud-Men were so flabbergasted at seeing one of their company carried away in this manner that they let go the ropes they were holding, and then of course down went the rainbow, both halves of it together, tumbling toward the earth below. This freed the peach, which at once began sailing away from that terrible cloud.

But the travelers were not in the clear yet. The infuriated Cloud-Men jumped up and ran after them along the cloud, pelting them mercilessly with all sorts of hard and horrible objects. Empty paint buckets, paint brushes, stepladders, stools, saucepans, frying-pans, rotten eggs, dead rats, bottles of hair-oil—anything those brutes could lay their hands on came raining down upon the peach. One Cloud-Man, taking very careful aim, tipped a gallon of thick purple paint over the edge of the cloud right onto the Centipede himself.

The Centipede screamed with anger. "My legs!" he cried. "They are all sticking together! I can't walk! And my eyelids won't open! I can't see! And my boots! My boots are ruined!"

But for the moment everyone was far too busy dodging the things that the Cloud-Men were throwing to pay any attention to the Centipede.

"The paint is drying!" he moaned. "It's going hard! I can't move my legs! I can't move anything!"

"You can still move your mouth," the Earthworm said. "And that is a great pity."

"James!" bawled the Centipede. "Please help me! Wash off this paint! Scrape it off! Anything!"

29

It seemed like a long time before the seagulls were able to pull the peach away from that horrible rainbow-cloud. But they managed it at last, and then everybody gathered around the wretched Centipede and began arguing about the best way to get the paint off his body.

He really did look a sight. He was purple all over, and now that the paint was beginning to dry and harden, he was forced to sit very stiff and upright, as though he were encased in cement. And all forty-two of his legs were sticking out straight in front of him, like rods. He tried to say something, but his lips wouldn't move. All he could do now was to make gurgling noises in his throat.

The Old-Green-Grasshopper reached out and touched him carefully on the stomach. "But how could it possibly have dried so quickly?" he asked.

"It's rainbow-paint," James answered. "Rainbow-paint dries very quick and very hard."

"I detest paint," Miss Spider announced. "It frightens me. It reminds me of Aunt Spiker—the *late* Aunt Spiker, I mean—because the last time she painted her kitchen ceiling my poor darling grandmother stepped into it by mistake when it was still wet, and there she stuck. And all through the night we could hear her calling to us, saying 'Help! help! help!' and it was heartbreaking to listen to her. But what could we do? Not a thing until the next day when the paint had dried, and then of course we all rushed over to her and calmed her down and gave her some food. Believe it or not, she lived for six months like that, upside down on the ceiling with her legs stuck permanently in the paint. She really did. We fed her every day. We brought her fresh flies straight from the web. But then on the twenty-sixth of April last, Aunt Sponge—the *late* Aunt Sponge, I mean—happened to glance up at the ceiling, and she spotted her. 'A spider!' she cried. 'A disgusting spider! Quick! Fetch me the mop with the long handle!' And then—Oh, it was so awful I can't bear to think of it...." Miss Spider wiped away a tear and looked sadly at the Centipede. "You poor thing," she murmured. "I do feel sorry for you."

"It'll never come off," the Earthworm said brightly. "Our Centipede will never move again. He will turn into a statue and we shall be able to put him in the middle of the lawn with a bird-bath on the top of his head."

"We could try peeling him like a banana," the Old-Green-Grasshopper suggested.

"Or rubbing him with sandpaper," the Ladybug said.

"Now if he stuck out his tongue," the Earthworm said, smiling a little for perhaps the first time in his life, "if he stuck it out really far, then we could all catch hold of it and start pulling. And if we pulled hard enough we could turn him inside out and he would have a new skin!"

There was a pause while the others considered this interesting proposal.

"I think," James said slowly, "I think that the best thing to do…" Then he stopped. "What was *that*?" he asked quickly. "I heard a voice! I heard someone shouting!"

30

They all raised their heads, listening.

"Ssshh! There it is again!"

But the voice was too far away for them to hear what it was saying.

"It's a Cloud-Man!" Miss Spider cried. "I just know it's a Cloud-Man! They're after us again!"

"It came from above!" the Earthworm said, and automatically everybody looked upward, everybody except the Centipede, who couldn't move.

"Ouch!" they said. "Help! Mercy! We're going to catch it this time!" For what they now saw, swirling and twisting directly over their heads, was an immense black cloud, a terrible, dangerous, thundery-looking thing that began to rumble and roar even as they were staring at it. And then, from high up on the top of the cloud, the faraway voice came down to them once again, this time very loud and clear.

"*On with the faucets!*" it shouted. "*On with the faucets! On with the faucets!*"

Three seconds later, the whole underneath of the cloud seemed to split and burst open like a paper bag, and then—

out came the water! They saw it coming. It was quite easy to see because it wasn't just raindrops. It wasn't raindrops at all. It was a great solid mass of water that might have been a lake or a whole ocean dropping out of the sky on top of them, and down it came, down and down and down, crashing first onto the seagulls and then onto the peach itself, while the poor travelers shrieked with fear and groped around frantically for something to catch hold of—the peach stem, the silk strings, anything they could find—and all the time the water came pouring and roaring down upon them, bouncing and smashing and sloshing and slashing and swashing and swirling and surging and whirling and gurgling and gushing and rushing and rushing, and it was like being pinned down underneath the biggest waterfall in the world and not being able to get out. They couldn't speak. They couldn't see. They couldn't breathe. And James Henry Trotter, holding on madly to one of the silk strings above the peach stem, told himself that this must surely be the end of everything at last. But then, just as suddenly as it had started, the deluge stopped. They were out of it and it was all over. The wonderful seagulls had flown right through it and had come out safely on the other side. Once again the giant peach was sailing peacefully through the mysterious moonlit sky.

"I am drowned!" gasped the Old-Green-Grasshopper, spitting out water by the pint.

"It's gone right through my skin!" the Earthworm groaned. "I always thought my skin was waterproof but it isn't and now I'm full of rain!"

"Look at me, look at me!" shouted the Centipede excitedly. "It's washed me *clean*! The paint's all gone! I can move again!"

"That's the worst news I've had in a long time," the Earthworm said.

The Centipede was dancing around the deck and turning somersaults in the air and singing at the top of his voice:

> "Oh, hooray for the storm and the rain!
> I can move! I don't feel any pain!
> And now I'm a pest,
> I'm the biggest and best,
> The most marvelous pest once again!"

> "Oh, do shut up," the Old-Green-Grasshopper said.
> "Look at me!" cried the Centipede.

> "Look at ME! I am freed! I am freed!
> Not a scratch nor a bruise nor a bleed!
> To his grave this fine gent
> They all thought they had sent
> And I very near went!
> Oh, I VERY near went!
> But they cent quite the wrong Sentipede!"

31

"How fast we are going all of a sudden," the Ladybug said. "I wonder why?"

"I don't think the seagulls like this place any better than we do," James answered. "I imagine they want to get out of it as soon as they can. They got a bad fright in the storm we've just been through."

Faster and faster flew the seagulls, skimming across the sky at a tremendous pace, with the peach trailing out behind them. Cloud after cloud went by on either side, all of them ghostly white in the moonlight, and several more times during the night the travelers caught glimpses of Cloud-Men moving around on the tops of these clouds, working their sinister magic upon the world below.

Once they passed a snow machine in operation, with the Cloud-Men turning the handle and a blizzard of snowflakes blowing out of the great funnel above. They saw the huge drums that were used for making thunder, and the Cloud-Men beating them furiously with long hammers. They saw the frost factories and the wind producers and the places where cyclones and tornadoes were manufactured and sent spinning down toward the Earth, and once, deep in the hollow of a large billowy cloud, they spotted something that could only have been a Cloud-Men's city. There were caves everywhere running into the cloud, and at the entrances to the caves the Cloud-Men's wives were crouching over little stoves with frying-pans in their hands, frying snowballs for their husbands' suppers. And hundreds of Cloud-Men's children were frisking about all over the place and shrieking with laughter and sliding down the billows of the cloud on toboggans.

An hour later, just before dawn, the travelers heard a soft *whooshing* noise above their heads and they glanced up and saw an immense gray batlike creature swooping down toward them out of the dark. It circled round and round the peach, flapping its great wings slowly in the moonlight and staring at the travelers. Then it uttered a series of long deep melancholy cries and flew off again into the night.

"Oh, I do wish the morning would come!" Miss Spider said, shivering all over.

"It won't be long now," James answered. "Look, it's getting lighter over there already."

They all sat in silence watching the sun as it came up slowly over the rim of the horizon for a new day.

32

And when full daylight came at last, they all got to their feet and stretched their poor cramped bodies, and then the Centipede, who always seemed to see things first, shouted, "Look! There's land below!"

"He's right!" they cried, running to the edge of the peach and peering over. "Hooray! Hooray!"

"It looks like streets and houses!"

"But how enormous it all is!"

A vast city, glistening in the early-morning sunshine, lay spread out three thousand feet below them. At that height, the cars were like little beetles crawling along the streets, and people walking on the pavements looked no larger than tiny grains of soot.

"But what tremendous tall buildings!" exclaimed the Ladybug. "I've never seen anything like *them* before in England. Which town do you think it is?"

"This couldn't possibly be England," said the Old-Green-Grasshopper.

"Then where is it?" asked Miss Spider.

"You know what those buildings are?" shouted James, jumping up and down with excitement. "Those are skyscrapers! So this must be America! And that, my friends, means that we have crossed the Atlantic Ocean overnight!"

"You don't mean it!" they cried.

"It's not possible!"

"It's incredible! It's unbelievable!"

"Oh, I've always dreamed of going to America!" cried the Centipede. "I had a friend once who—"

"Be quiet!" said the Earthworm. "Who cares about your friend? The thing we've got to think about now is *how on earth are we going to get down to earth?*"

"Ask James," said the Ladybug.

"I don't think that should be so very difficult," James told them. "All we'll have to do is to cut loose a few seagulls. Not too many, mind you, but just enough so that the others can't *quite* keep us up in the air. Then down we shall go, slowly and gently, until we reach the ground. Centipede will bite through the strings for us one at a time."

33

Far below them, in the City of New York, something like pandemonium was breaking out. A great round ball as big as a house had been sighted hovering high up in the sky over the very center of Manhattan, and the cry had gone up that it was an enormous bomb sent over by another country to blow the whole city to smithereens. Air-raid sirens began wailing in every section. All radio and television programs were interrupted with announcements that the population must go down into their cellars immediately. One million people walking in the streets on their way to work looked up into the sky and saw the monster hovering above them, and started running for the nearest subway entrance to take cover. Generals grabbed hold of telephones and shouted orders to everyone they could think of. The Mayor of New York called up the President of the United States down in Washington, D.C., to ask him for help, and the President, who at that moment was having breakfast in his pajamas, quickly pushed away his half-finished plate of Sugar Crisps and started pressing buttons right and left to summon his Admirals and his Generals. And all the way across the vast stretch of America, in all the fifty States from Alaska to Florida, from Pennsylvania to Hawaii, the alarm was sounded and the word went out that the biggest bomb in the history of the world was hovering over New York City, and that at any moment it might go off.

34

"Come on, Centipede, bite through the first string," James ordered.

The Centipede took one of the silk strings between his teeth and bit through it. And once again (but *not* with an angry Cloud-Man dangling from the end of the string this time) a single seagull came away from the rest of the flock and went flying off on its own.

"Bite another," James ordered.

The Centipede bit through another string.

"Why aren't we sinking?"

"We are sinking!"

"No, we're not!"

"Don't forget the peach is a lot lighter now than when we started out," James told them. "It lost an awful lot of juice when all those hailstones hit it in the night. Cut away two more seagulls, Centipede!"

"Ah, that's better!"

"Here we go!"

"Now we really are sinking!"

"Yes, this is perfect! Don't bite any more, Centipede, or we'll sink too fast! Gently does it!"

Slowly the great peach began losing height, and the buildings and streets down below began coming closer and closer.

"Do you think we'll all get our pictures in the papers when we get down?" the Ladybug asked.

"My goodness, I've forgotten to polish my boots!" the

Centipede said. "Everyone must help me to polish my boots before we arrive."

"Oh, for heaven's sake!" said the Earthworm. "Can't you ever stop thinking about—"

But he never finished his sentence. For suddenly... *WHOOOSH!*...and they looked up and saw a huge four-engined plane come shooting out of a nearby cloud and go whizzing past them not more than twenty feet over their heads. This was actually the regular early-morning passenger plane coming in to New York from Chicago, and as it went by, it sliced right through every single one of the silken strings, and immediately the seagulls broke away, and the enormous peach, having nothing to hold it up in the air any longer, went tumbling down toward the earth like a lump of lead.

"Help!" cried the Centipede.

"Save us!" cried Miss Spider.

"We are lost!" cried the Ladybug.

"This is the end!" cried the Old-Green-Grasshopper.

"James!" cried the Earthworm. "Do something, James! Quickly, do something!"

"I can't!" cried James. "I'm sorry! Good-by! Shut your eyes, everybody! It won't be long now!"

35

Round and round and upside down went the peach as it plummeted toward the earth, and they were all clinging desperately to the stem to save themselves from being flung into space.

Faster and faster it fell. Down and down and down, racing closer and closer to the houses and streets below, where it would surely smash into a million pieces when it hit. And all the way along Fifth Avenue and Madison Avenue, and along all the other streets in the City, people who had not yet reached the underground shelters looked up and saw it coming, and they stopped running and stood there staring in a sort of stupor at what they thought was the biggest bomb in all the world falling out of the sky onto their heads. A few women screamed. Others knelt down on the sidewalks and began praying aloud. Strong men turned to one another and said things like, "I guess this is it, Joe," and "Good-by, everybody, good-by." And for the next thirty seconds the whole City held its breath, waiting for the end to come.

36

"Good-by, Ladybug!" gasped James, clinging to the stem of the falling peach. "Good-by, Centipede. Good-by, everybody!" There were only a few seconds to go now and it looked as though they were going to fall right in among all the tallest buildings. James could see the skyscrapers rushing up to meet them at the most awful speed, and most of them had square flat tops, but the very tallest of them all had a top that tapered off into a long sharp point—like an enormous silver needle sticking up into the sky.

And it was precisely onto the top of this needle that the peach fell!

There was a squelch. The needle went in deep. And suddenly—there was the giant peach, caught and spiked upon the very pinnacle of the Empire State Building.

37

It was really an amazing sight, and in two or three minutes, as soon as the people below realized that this now couldn't possibly be a bomb, they came pouring out of the shelters and the subways to gape at the marvel. The streets for half a mile around the building were jammed with men and women, and when the word spread that there were actually living things moving about on the top of the great round ball, then everyone went wild with excitement.

"It's a flying saucer!" they shouted.

"They are from Outer Space!"

"They are men from Mars!"

"Or maybe they came from the Moon!"

And a man who had a pair of binoculars to his eyes said, "They look *pritt*-ty peculiar to me, I'll tell you that."

Police cars and fire engines came screaming in from all over the city and pulled up outside the Empire State Building. Two hundred firemen and six hundred policemen swarmed into the building and went up in the elevators as high as they could go. Then they poured out onto the observation roof—which is the place where tourists stand—just at the bottom of the big spike.

All the policemen were holding their guns at the ready, with their fingers on the triggers, and the firemen were clutching their hatchets. But from where they stood, almost directly underneath the peach, they couldn't actually see the travelers up on top.

"Ahoy there!" shouted the Chief of Police. "Come out and show yourselves!"

Suddenly, the great brown head of the Centipede appeared over the side of the peach. His black eyes, as large and round as two marbles, glared down at the policemen and the firemen below. Then his monstrous ugly face broke into a wide grin.

The policemen and the firemen all started shouting at once. "Look out!" they cried. "It's a Dragon!"

"It's not a Dragon! It's a Wampus!"

"It's a Gorgon!"

"It's a Sea-serpent!"

"It's a Prock!"

"It's a Manticore!"

Three firemen and five policemen fainted and had to be carried away.

"It's a Snozzwanger!" cried the Chief of Police.

"It's a Whangdoodle!" yelled the Head of the Fire Department.

The Centipede kept on grinning. He seemed to be enjoying enormously the commotion that he was causing.

"Now see here!" shouted the Chief of Police, cupping his hands to his mouth. "You listen to me! I want you to tell me exactly where you've come from!"

"We've come from thousands of miles away!" the Centipede shouted back, grinning more broadly than ever and showing his brown teeth.

"There you are!" cried the Chief of Police. "I *told* you they came from Mars!"

"I guess you're right!" said the Head of the Fire Department.

At this point, the Old-Green-Grasshopper poked his huge green head over the side of the peach, alongside the Centipede's. Six more big strong men fainted when they saw him.

"That one's an Oinck!" screamed the Head of the Fire Department. "I just *know* it's an Oinck!"

"Or a Cockatrice!" yelled the Chief of Police. "Stand back, men! It may jump down on us any moment!"

"What on earth are they talking about?" the Old-Green-Grasshopper said to the Centipede.

"Search me," the Centipede answered. "But they seem to be in an awful stew about something."

Then Miss Spider's large black murderous-looking head, which to a stranger was probably the most terrifying of all, appeared next to the Grasshopper's.

"Snakes and ladders!" yelled the Head of the Fire Department. "We are finished now! It's a giant Scorpula!"

"It's worse than that!" cried the Chief of Police. "It's a vermicious Knid! Oh, just look at its vermicious gruesome face!"

"Is that the kind that eats fully grown men for breakfast?" the Head of the Fire Department asked, going white as a sheet.

"I'm afraid it is," the Chief of Police answered.

"Oh, *please* why doesn't someone help us to get down from here?" Miss Spider called out. "It's making me giddy."

"This could be a trick!" said the Head of the Fire Department. "Don't anyone make a move until I say!"

"They've probably got space guns!" muttered the Chief of Police.

"But we've *got* to do *something*!" the Head of the Fire

Department announced grimly. "About five million people are standing down there on the streets watching us."

"Then why don't you put up a ladder?" the Chief of Police asked him. "I'll stand at the bottom and hold it steady for you while you go up and see what's happening."

"Thanks very much!" snapped the Head of the Fire Department.

Soon there were no less than *seven* large fantastic faces peering down over the side of the peach—the Centipede's, the Old-Green-Grasshopper's, Miss Spider's, the Earthworm's, the Ladybug's, the Silkworm's, and the Glow-worm's. And a sort of panic was beginning to break out among the firemen and the policemen on the rooftop.

Then, all at once, the panic stopped and a great gasp of astonishment went up all around. For now, a small boy was seen to be standing up there beside the other creatures. His hair was blowing in the wind, and he was laughing and waving and calling out, "Hello, everybody! Hello!"

For a few moments, the men below just stood and stared and gaped. They simply couldn't believe their eyes.

"*Bless* my soul!" cried the Head of the Fire Department, going red in the face. "It really is a little boy, isn't it?"

"Don't be frightened of us, please!" James called out. "We are so glad to be here!"

"What about those others beside you?" shouted the Chief of Police. "Are any of them dangerous?"

"Of course they're not dangerous!" James answered. "They're the nicest creatures in the world! Allow me to introduce them to you one by one and then I'm sure you will believe me.

"My friends, this is the Centipede, and let me make
        it known
He is so sweet and gentle that (although he's
            overgrown)
The Queen of Spain, again and again, has
            summoned him by phone
To baby-sit and sing and knit and be a chaperone
When nurse is off and all the royal children are all
            alone."
("Small wonder," said a Fireman, "they're no longer
        on the throne.")

"The Earthworm, on the other hand,"
Said James, beginning to expand,
"Is great for digging up the land
And making old soils newer.
Moreover, you should understand
He would be absolutely grand
For digging subway tunnels and
For making you a sewer."
(The Earthworm blushed and beamed with pride.
Miss Spider clapped and cheered and cried,
"Could any words be truer?")

"And the Grasshopper, ladies and gents, is a boon
In millions and millions of ways.
You have only to ask him to give you a tune
And he plays and he plays and he plays.
As a toy for your children he's perfectly sweet;
There's nothing so good in the shops—
You've only to tickle the soles of his feet
And he hops and he hops and he hops."
("He can't be very fierce!" exclaimed
The Head of all the Cops.)

"And now without excuse
I'd like to introduce
This charming Glow-worm, lover of simplicity.
She is easy to install
On your ceiling or your wall,
And although this smacks a bit of eccentricity,
It's really rather clever
For thereafter you will never
You will NEVER NEVER NEVER
Have the slightest need for using electricity."
(At which, no less than fifty-two
Policemen cried, "If this is true
That creature'll get some fabulous publicity!")

"And here we have Miss Spider
With a mile of thread inside her
Who has personally requested me to say
That she's NEVER *met Miss Muffet*
On her charming little tuffet—
If she had she'd NOT *have frightened her away.*
Should her looks sometimes alarm you
Then I don't think it would harm you
To repeat at least a hundred times a day:
'I must NEVER *kill a spider*
I must only help and guide her
And invite her in the nursery to play.'"
(The Police all nodded slightly,
And the Firemen smiled politely,
And about a dozen people cried,
"Hooray!")

"And here's my darling Ladybug, so beautiful,
so kind,
My greatest comfort since this trip began.
She has four hundred children and she's left them
all behind,
But they're coming on the next peach if they can."
(The Cops cried, "She's entrancing!"
All the Firemen started dancing,
And the crowds all started cheering to a man!)

"And now, the Silkworm," James went on,
"Whose silk will bear comparison
With all the greatest silks there are
In Rome and Philadelphia.
If you would search the whole world through
From Paraguay to Timbuctoo
I don't think you would find one bit
Of silk that could compare with it.
Even the shops in Singapore
Don't have the stuff. And what is more,
This Silkworm had, I'll have you know,
The honor, not so long ago,
To spin and weave and sew and press
The Queen of England's wedding dress.
And she's already made and sent
A waistcoat for your President."
("Well, good for her!" the Cops cried out,
And all at once a mighty shout
Went up around the Empire State,
"Let's get them down at once! Why WAIT?")

38

Five minutes later, they were all safely down, and James was excitedly telling his story to a group of flabbergasted officials.

And suddenly—everyone who had come over on the peach was a hero! They were all escorted to the steps of City Hall, where the Mayor of New York made a speech of welcome. And while he was doing this, one hundred steeplejacks, armed with ropes and ladders and pulleys, swarmed up to the top of the Empire State Building and lifted the giant peach off the spike and lowered it to the ground.

Then the Mayor shouted, "We must now have a ticker-tape parade for our wonderful visitors!"

And so a procession was formed, and in the leading car (which was an enormous open limousine) sat James and all his friends.

Next came the giant peach itself. Men with cranes and hooks had quickly hoisted it onto a very large truck and there it now sat, looking just as huge and proud and brave as ever. There was, of course, a bit of a hole in the bottom of it where the spike of the Empire State Building had gone in, but who cared about that—or indeed about the peach juice that was dripping out of it onto the street?

Behind the peach, skidding about all over the place in the peach juice, came the Mayor's limousine, and behind the Mayor's limousine came about twenty other limousines carrying all the important people of the City.

And the crowds went wild with excitement. They leaned out of the windows of the skyscrapers, cheering and yelling and screaming and clapping and throwing out bits of white paper and ticker-tape, and James and his friends stood up in their car and waved back at them as they went by.

Then a rather curious thing happened. The procession was moving slowly along Fifth Avenue when suddenly a little girl in a red dress ran out from the crowd and shouted, "Oh, James, James! Could I *please* have just a tiny taste of your marvelous peach?"

"Help yourself!" James shouted back. "Eat all you want! It won't keep forever, anyway!"

No sooner had he said this than about fifty other children exploded out of the crowd and came running onto the street.

"Can *we* have some, too?" they cried.

"Of course you can!" James answered. "Everyone can have some!"

The children jumped up onto the truck and swarmed like ants all over the giant peach, eating and eating to their hearts' content. And as the news of what was happening spread quickly from street to street, more and more boys and girls came running from all directions to join the feast. Soon, there was a trail of children a mile long chasing after the peach as it proceeded slowly up Fifth Avenue. Really, it was a fantastic sight. To some people it looked as though the Pied Piper of Hamelin had suddenly descended upon New York. And to James, who had never dreamed that there could be so many children as this in the world, it was the most marvelous thing that had ever happened.

By the time the procession was over, the whole gigantic fruit had been completely eaten up, and only the big brown stone in the middle, licked clean and shiny by ten thousand eager little tongues, was left standing on the truck.

39

And thus the journey ended. But the travelers lived on. Every one of them became rich and successful in the new country.

The Centipede was made Vice-President-in-Charge-of-Sales of a high-class firm of boot and shoe manufacturers.

The Earthworm, with his lovely pink skin, was employed by a company that made women's face creams to speak commercials on television.

The Silkworm and Miss Spider, after they had both been taught to make nylon thread instead of silk, set up a factory together and made ropes for tightrope walkers.

The Glow-worm became the light inside the torch on the Statue of Liberty, and thus saved a grateful City from having to pay a huge electricity bill every year.

The Old-Green-Grasshopper became a member of the New York Symphony Orchestra, where his playing was greatly admired.

The Ladybug, who had been haunted all her life by the fear that her house was on fire and her children all gone, married the Head of the Fire Department and lived happily ever after.

And as for the enormous peach stone—it was set up permanently in a place of honor in Central Park and became a famous monument. But it was not *only* a famous monument. It was also a famous house. And inside the famous house there lived a famous person—

JAMES HENRY TROTTER
himself.

And all you had to do any day of the week was to go and knock upon the door, and the door would always be opened to you, and you would always be asked to come inside and see the famous room where James had first met his friends. And sometimes, if you were very lucky, you would find the Old-Green-Grasshopper in there as well, resting peacefully in a chair before the fire, or perhaps it would be the Ladybug who had dropped in for a cup of tea and a gossip, or the Centipede to show off a new batch of particularly elegant boots that he had just acquired.

Every day of the week, hundreds and hundreds of children from far and near came pouring into the City to see the marvelous peach stone in the Park. And James Henry Trotter, who once, if you remember, had been the saddest and loneliest little boy that you could find, now had all the friends and playmates in the world. And because so many of them were always begging him to tell and tell again the story of his adventures on the peach, he thought it would be nice if one day he sat down and wrote a book.

So he did.

And *that* is what you have just finished reading.

ABOUT THE AUTHOR

Roald Dahl was born in Wales in 1916 of Norwegian parents. He grew up in England and lived there until his death in 1990. At the onset of World War II, he joined the Royal Air Force and became a fighter pilot. His career as a writer began in 1946, when his first collection of short stories for adults was published, but it was not until 1961, when his first book for children—*James and the Giant Peach*—was published, that he found his true calling. Dahl wrote more than a dozen children's books, including *Charlie and the Chocolate Factory, Danny: The Champion of the World, The B.F.G.,* and *Matilda.* Together, they made him one of the most popular writers of children's books in the world. His books stand as modern fairy tales in which powerless children triumph over evil adults. He is widely acknowledged as a literary genius who changed children's literature forever.

ABOUT THE ILLUSTRATOR

Lane Smith was born in Oklahoma in 1959 and received a B.F.A. degree from Art Center College of Design in Pasadena, California. His work appeared on many magazine covers and book jackets and in numerous newspapers before he found children's books the ideal showcase for his irreverent, childlike sense of humor. Among his books are *The True Story of the Three Little Pigs, The Stinky Cheese Man,* which was a Caldecott Honor Book, and *Math Curse,* all written by Jon Scieszka, as well as *The Big Pets* and *The Happy Hocky Family,* which Smith both wrote and illustrated. His visual interpretation of the characters and settings in *James and the Giant Peach* was used by Disney as the basis for the animation in the 1996 feature film. He lives in New York City.

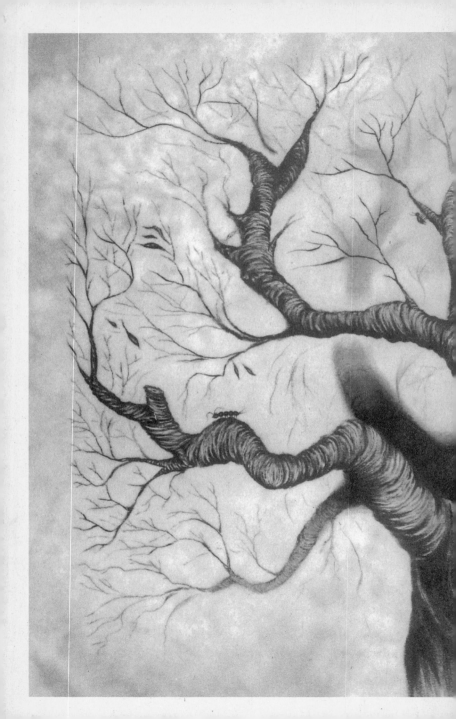